Edmund Downey

In One Town

A novel. Vol. 1

Edmund Downey

In One Town
A novel. Vol. 1

ISBN/EAN: 9783337066734

Printed in Europe, USA, Canada, Australia, Japan

Cover: Foto ©Andreas Hilbeck / pixelio.de

More available books at **www.hansebooks.com**

IN ONE TOWN.

A NOVEL.

BY

THE AUTHOR OF
"ANCHOR-WATCH YARNS," ETC.

" Many ways meet in one town."— *King Henry V.*

IN TWO VOLUMES.

VOL. I.

LONDON:
WARD & DOWNEY,
12 YORK STREET, COVENT GARDEN.

1886.

CONTENTS.

Part the Second.

A MESSAGE FROM THE DEEP.

IN ONE TOWN. .

IN ONE TOWN.

PROLOGUE.

ONE evening, late in August, a young
man stood on a wooden bridge which
spanned a broad river. He was lean-
ing with folded arms against the parapet of the
drawbridge, gazing dreamingly at the quivering
belt of light which the sun, sinking redly behind
a western hill, sent across the unruffled waters.
The tide was still flowing, but the flood was well-
nigh spent, for no motion seemed to disturb the
waters. The day had been calm and sultry, but
with the going down of the sun a soft breeze came
up from the south.

The traffic on the bridge had almost ceased; occasionally a foot-passenger went by, and from some small pleasure boats which passed at intervals under the drawbridge, the hum of conversation, and the clank of oars in their rowlocks, reached the young man's ears.

He turned round as the refulgence died out of the waters, and walked to the opposite side of the bridge. Here he leant against the parapet, and stood gazing down the stream. In front of him lay a long stretch of river, and on each side of the river was shipping. A few vessels rode at anchor in the channel, and when the sun had set, their anchor lights, pale and indistinct, were hoisted into the dusky rigging. Along the quays on both sides the lamps were being slowly light, and like stars breaking through the early night came the lights from the windows of the houses built on the slopes rising from the quays. In the south, behind the lines of shipping, a heavy, low-lying bank of cloud hung like a pall in mid air.

For some time the young man remained almost motionless. Half unconsciously he was drinking in the quiet beauty of the scene. With the ebbing of the tide the boats ceased to go up the stream, and no sound now reached his ears save the rhythmic ripple of the river as it licked the wooden piers of the bridge.

Lifting his head, he was surprised to find that night was rapidly setting in—he had not observed the growth of the darkness until he saw the pale stars overhead. As he looked again down the stream, the lights on the quays and the lights from the houses on the hillsides seemed to have grown suddenly deeper and fuller.

Taking out his watch, he thought, "It must be near nine o'clock."

It wanted a quarter of the hour.

"It may be many, many years," he moodily reflected, "until I shall look upon the dear old river again. Perhaps I may not come back to it until I have grown old and world-worn, and then I shall stand here once more, and think of all the days I have passed within sight of it, and of all the delicious hours I have spent paddling up and down and across it. Perhaps I may never see it again—but no! I could not die happy if I were to die away from you, old river," he murmured, stretching out his arms embracingly. "Bah!" he cried, drawing back his arms, a big sob ready to burst from his compressed lips, "I am growing maudlin."

He dashed his hand .across his eyes, and looking down the stream, watched the blurred lights— for his eyes were wet with tears—from the lamps along the quays, the reflections from many of them finding their way into the river, and sending long spears of dull yellow flame out into the stream. The cloud bank in the south had grown denser and blacker, and was moving menacingly towards him, blotting out the stars in its progress.

The ebb tide had been gradually gathering strength, and was gurgling rapidly through the openings of the bridge. The murmur of voices from the river, and the clank, now clear and ringing, from the oars in the rowlocks of boats returning with the tide, drew the young man's attention from his gloomy musings. Now and then the sound of music and of laughter from the boats as they passed beneath him caused a smile to flit across his face. He had again forgotten the lapse of time, when the melancholy boom of the town clock sounded in his ears and startled him.

"Nine!" he cried, as the last echo of the clock died away.

It was quite dark, and the night air had grown chilly. No one had crossed the bridge for over a quarter of an hour. He looked around him. He tried to convince himself that he heard every moment the hollow sounds of approaching foot-steps. He peered through the darkness, and every moment he fancied he could distinguish a well-known figure advancing towards him along the bridge, which seemed now like some shrub-bordered avenue. He was fast growing impatient. Could anything have happened? Surely she would not disappoint him wilfully on this—the last night? No. This was she at last! He could not be mistaken this time.

He walked rapidly towards her.

"My darling Susie!" he cried, seizing her hands, "I had almost given up all hope of seeing you."

"Have you been waiting long, Dick?"

"I think I have been here an hour, perhaps two hours. Really I could not tell you how long. Of

course, I did not expect you before nine, darling;
but I thought I would spend my last night here
in company of my old friend the river."

"And are you really going away in the morning, Dick? I can't believe I am to see you no
more for months and months. But perhaps you
are glad to be going away," she pouted. "You
seem quite happy."

"Yes, ever so happy while you are near me,"
pressing her gloved hand and raising it to his
lips. Then with a mingling of bitterness and
sadness in his voice, "And yet it seems almost
inhuman that I could be light-hearted even for a
moment after—after what has happened."

They now reached the drawbridge.

" I have been very low-spirited all the day,
Susie," he said, drawing her gently towards the
parapet. "I have been standing here since the
sun went down, full of all sorts of gloomy
memories and dark forebodings."

"The river at night always makes me sad,
too," she murmured. "I should be afraid to cross
the bridge after dark. Listen, Dick, to the
water rushing through the piers. All night that

noise will be in my ears. It makes me quite nervous to listen to it," she cried, with a slight shiver.

"Oh, don't blame the dear old river! I won't let anyone say a word against it. It has too many pleasant memories for me. Susie, my darling," he cried, swiftly seizing both her hands, and looking ardently into her dark, luminous eyes, "will you ever forget me; will you ever cease to care for me?"

The girl cast down her eyes, and drawing her right hand from his clasp, and laying it tenderly on his right hand, she whispered,—

"Why need you ask me that, Dick; you know I will never, never forget you."

"My own darling!" he cried, pressing both her hands; then in a quieter and graver tone, "but suppose I were to be a very, very long time away from you; suppose I did not get on in the world; suppose it were years and years—never is such a long time," he smiled sadly—"before I could come back to claim you—would you still be true to me?"

"You will be much more likely to forget me,

than I to forget you. But you won't be very long away, Dick, will you?" she asked tearfully.

"Not longer than I can help, you may be quite sure; but, indeed, darling, my future does not look very rosy just now. We must both have hope and courage, I suppose."

"You look so solemn now, Dick," she murmured. Then, after a little pause, "You have made my hands so hot. Do, please, let them go."

He released them at once. He wanted ever so much to take her in his arms and kiss her; but he had never attempted to kiss her, and he feared she would repulse him. Why should she snatch her hands away from him? He could never understand girls. In a somewhat careless tone he said,—

"I suppose you must soon go home, Susie? It must be near ten now. I hope I shall not be the means of getting you into trouble with your mother. I would not have pressed you to come here tonight, only I could not bear the thought of parting from you in your own house; your mother's eyes never seem to leave me while I am near you.

If I had known, though, that your good-bye would have been such a cold one, I would not have asked you to meet me here."

"You are vexed now, Dick," she whispered, looking up at him with half-closed eyes. "What have I done to vex you? It is you who are cold, not I."

He glanced swiftly at her. Then in a moment his arms were round her, and he kissed her passionately on lips, eyes, and cheek.

When he released her, she sighed, and, placing one hand caressingly on his cheek, asked, in a low, tremulous whisper,—

"Did you ever kiss anyone before, Dick — I mean anyone like—like me?"

"Never, my darling!" he cried. Then, taking her white, plump hands, and holding them on his shoulders, he said, "Now, Susie, dearest, look me straight in the eyes, and tell me that you love me, and will never, never love anybody else. Say it to me, dearest."

"I love you, my darling Dick"—and then, ashamed of her boldness, she hung her head.

"My beauty!" he murmured. Clasping her once more round the waist, he bent down, and, placing his lips close to her ear, cried,—"I love you! I love you! I love you!"

The boom of the town clock startled them. To both it sounded like a knell.

"There, Dick, dearest, let me go," she cried nervously. "That is ten o'clock striking; I did not think it was so late. Is that rain?"

He held out his hand; a few heavy raindrops fell one by one on the palm. Looking up at the sky he found that the stars were no longer visible. The cloud had come up from the south, and stretching itself out, had made the night supremely dark. The river seemed like a great dull sheet of bronze, the reflection from the lamps on the quays looking like dimly-polished patches on the metal. The distant lights from the quiet town and the anchor lights of the vessels were fainter and duller.

"I fear there will be a rainstorm before long," he said. "You must get home at once. Come, dearest."

Taking her hand caressingly, he drew her arm through his, and they walked hurriedly along the bridge.

"You were vexed with me a while ago, Dick," she whispered, leaning her head against his shoulder, and looking up at him, "because I took my hands away. I think I was almost going to kiss you then myself."

He stared at her in amazement.

"Yes," she went on, "you must think me too forward and wicked, Dick; but I may not see you again for so long—and I could not bear the thought of parting from you without a kiss; and do you know, Dick, I thought it would be so strange and so cold to keep my gloves on! That was why I took my hands away, Dick."

"My darling!" he cried rapturously.

They were now approaching the gate of the bridge, and for a moment they stood still. He was in such a whirl of intoxication that he could only stare in wonderment at the young face so temptingly near him. He knew he had many things to say, many questions to ask, many plans to arrange; but he could not formulate his thoughts into words.

"You would never have kissed me," she murmured—"I mean really kissed me—if I had not almost asked you. Would you, Dick?"

He blushed deeply and stammered.

"I don't know—I was half afraid of you—oh, my darling, darling little girl! I will kiss you now, though—do, dearest, for the last time, before the sound of the river dies out in our ears."

. . . .

Part the First.

THE SAILING OF THE SHIP.

CHAPTER I.

DESCRIBES AN OLD-FASHIONED SEAPORT, AND A STORMY INTERVIEW.

LOUGHFORD was an oddly-built, old-fashioned seaport town in the south of Ireland. It was situated some dozen miles from the mouth of a broad river, the Slough, which flowed alongside the town almost due east and west, and, for a considerable distance higher up than the town, was navigable for ships of large tonnage. The quay at the southern side of the river was about a mile in length, and represented the base of an equilateral triangle with regard to the town itself; and from it there was a gradual ascent until the summit of a hill some five hundred feet above the level of the river was reached.

This quay was wide, and along it were built houses of various sizes and various styles of architecture. No one house resembled another; each possessed a distinct individuality of its own. A four-storey house, the ground floor a grocer's shop, might be found, flanked on one side by a two-storey building, the ground floor a nautical instrument maker's shop, and on the other side by a large ungainly - looking building — a corn store— studded with innumerable small window frames, whose wooden shutters, painted a dull, heavy brown, did duty for glass.

There was no private dwelling - house on the quay; every building was either a shop, a store, or an office. Where a fascia board appeared over a shop window, the proprietor took care to announce that he appealed chiefly to seafarers. The grocer had "Ship's stores supplied here," painted over his window; the draper, "Seamen's apparel of all sorts at cost prices;" the baker, "Ship's biscuits—best quality;" the butcher, "Prime beef and pork for ship's use." Even the one vendor of agricultural implements, who dwelt on the quay, made it known that there was a forge at the back of his premises for the use of vessels. The principal coal and corn stores were also situated on the quay, and, almost as a matter of course, the Custom House.

Parallel with the quay, a little higher up in the town, was a long street, called Princes Street, and here the nautical element was considerably toned down. The shops in Princes Street were patronised chiefly by the resident population and by the farming classes. There were several private dwelling-houses here, tenanted by those who had business in the stores or offices on the quay.

In the more elevated part of the seaport dwelt the dealers in pigs and cattle, and the shopkeepers who lived chiefly by them and by the farmers who visited the town on market days; but as this story will attempt to deal only with the maritime element, there is no occasion to linger in this purely terrestrial quarter.

On the outskirts of Sloughford at the western end were a number of straggling streets grouped together in a higgledy - piggledy fashion. The streets consisted mainly of thatched cottages, and low two-storey houses, some of them in a woefully dilapidated condition. These houses were tenanted by labourers, who for the most part worked on the quay; 'long-shore folk who made out, somehow, a precarious living amongst the shipping; artisans; and a sprinkling of cattle-dealers and shopkeepers. This suburb was neither wholly outside the bounds of Sloughford, nor wholly within them, and was known as "Yellow Hill," a title it probably derived from the fact that the soil was yellow clay. Yellow Hill was situated on the highest land about the town, and almost overhung the river above the bridge. In many places ruins of old Danish castles and fortifications might be seen, and on the summit of the hill three sides of a large Anglo - Norman castle stood almost intact.

On the outskirts of the town, at the eastern end, was the aristocratic suburb of River View. The houses here were all of a modern type, and were more showy-looking than any of the buildings in Sloughford town. Here dwelt merchants and ship-owners who were wealthy, or supposed to be wealthy.

Along the river bank, on the side opposite to Sloughford, ran a long, narrow quay, lined with large warehouses, stores, and timber yards. There were a few dwelling-houses at this side of the river, which was called Bankside, and in one of them, Woodbine Cottage, dwelt Captain John M'Cormick's wife—it could scarcely be called the residence of Captain M'Cormick, for even when his ship lay in the Slough, the master of the *Water Nymph* not unfrequently took up his quarters in the cabin of the ship.

As at the Sloughford side of the river, there was a gradual slope in the ground at Bankside, and . the front windows of Woodbine Cottage, which was built about midway up the slope of the hill, commanded an almost uninterrupted view for two or three miles of the windings of the river to the eastward.

Bankside was connected with Sloughford by a wooden bridge, the entrance to which, at the town side, was at the extreme upper end of the quay. During the daytime there was a considerable and continuous traffic across the wooden bridge, as the most fertile portion of the country

lay at the Bankside part of the river, and there
was no other means of approaching Sloughford
from the opposite side except by crossing the
bridge — the only one which spanned the river
for twenty miles from its mouth.

Standing on the bridge and gazing down the
river, it would be impossible not to be struck by
the fantastic appearance of Sloughford—the long
line of ships at either side of the river, stretching
itself almost as far as the eye could reach, for at
the lower end of the quay an abrupt bend in the
river shut out a further view of the stream—the
long line of oddly-grouped houses at the town
side, dimly visible through a tangled network
of rigging—the disjointed, uneven line of stores
at Bankside, buildings which could exist nowhere
but in a maritime town, and which seemed im-
pregnated with a weird nautical spirit. And on
a still summer evening, when the sun was sinking
behind Yellow Hill, its last red rays glancing
along the polished spars of the shipping at Bankside and lighting up the old-fashioned window
panes of the houses until the narrow panes seemed
so many tongues of flame, you would fain close your

eyes, and listening to the ripple of the river, fancy you had left the busy haunts of men behind you, and had been favoured with some old-world vision, strangely beautiful, and full of peace.

At the upper end of the southern quay, not far from the entrance to the wooden bridge, stood the "Bold Dragoon," a public-house whose history was lost in the mist of ages. A local historian had on one occasion unearthed documents which purported to give an account of Sloughford during the Cromwellian era. Prior to the occupation of the seaport by the Protector the public house had been in existence, and, according to the local historian, was identical with a well-known house of entertainment called the "Jolly Sailors." Sloughford had offered a determined resistance to the Cromwellians, and in the end had capitulated on honourable terms. One of the Roundhead troopers was afflicted with an inordinate thirst, and as soon as his company entered the town he rushed headlong to the nearest hostelry, which happened to be this "Jolly Sailors." While slaking his thirst he discovered that the landlady was a remarkably handsome woman, and the trooper instantly fell head over ears in love with her. He asked a few questions, learned she was a widow, proposed, and was married to the lady within a week. Then, bidding defiance to the nautical patrons of the house, he took down the old sign of the "Jolly Sailors," and got a brand-new one painted—a portrait of himself on horseback in full fig. This legend was generally accepted, but there were other theories propounded with regard to the origin of the sign. At all events the weather-beaten horse and horseman painted on the board which swung and creaked over the door of the public-house had certainly seen many summers and winters go by.

The present landlady of the " Bold Dragoon " was Miss Julia Walsh. She was a half-sister of a certain Captain John M'Cormick, of whom mention has already been made, and who will figure prominently in the earlier portion of this story. Miss Walsh had entered into occupation about five years before her half-brother had elec-trified Sloughford by declaring himself the accepted suitor of a young lady who lived inside a social circle where, it was supposed, the pluckiest master-mariner would not dream of finding a breathing space.

Under the preceding *régime* the " Bold Dragoon " had fallen into ill-repute, and was the resort of the lowest class of sailors and 'longshore folk, who were supplied with drink so vile that the local authorities had been obliged to interfere, and had refused to grant a renewal of the licence. The house had then been shut up and offered for sale. M'Cormick, who was a shrewder man of business than sailors usually are, purchased the interest in the lease for a small sum. Then he brought influence to bear on the local magistrates, and guaranteed to remodel the premises, structurally and morally, if a new licence were granted to his sister. He obtained the licence with some difficulty, and he carried out his promise faithfully.

When the " Bold Dragoon " again opened its doors to the public, it was altogether a reformed place of entertainment for man and beast. Neither M'Cormick nor his sister knew anything about the business of a public-house, and for a few years they had to submit to being plundered by every

one—customers, tradespeople, and attendants. But
Miss Walsh did not despair, and gradually the
business began to work smoothly and profitably.
The brightness and cleanliness of the house under
the new management were almost sufficient to
scare away the class who had previously supported the " Bold Dragoon," and after a short
time it became the resort of a superior class of
customers—the coasting and foreign skippers and
mates, and a sprinkling of the farmers who came
to town on market days, and who possessed a
keen scent for " a good drop."

One room was set apart for the sole use of
the coasting master-mariners and their friends,
and another for the foreign skippers. The former
was known to seafarers as the " Nest ; " and as
it is only with the " Nest " this veracious chronicle
will occasionally have business, it will be unnecessary to describe the apartment rendered sacred to
the foreign mariners.

The Nest was a long, low-ceilinged room behind
the shop, the entrance being through a short, narrow passage at one end of the counter. The doorway
—the door itself stood generally wide open—faced

the only window in the room. A deal table, carefully scoured every morning, occupied the centre of the floor, and two long moveable forms lay at either side of the table. There was a large old-fashioned fireplace at the far end of the room, with an open space in front capable of accommodating about half a dozen chairs. A few maps and charts decorated the white-washed walls, and an old barometer, an heirloom in the M'Cornick family, was hung near the doorway.

Julia Walsh was about thirty-eight years of age. Like her brother, she was tall and large boned; but, unlike him, she was thin and sharp-visaged. She believed herself to be a woman placed by circumstances altogether out of her natural sphere, but she knew the wisdom of pocketing her pride; and as she always lived in the hope that the "Bold Dragoon" would be hers after her brother's death, and as it was virtually hers while he lived, she did her best to make herself popular with her customers, without, however, unbending too much.

The majority of the frequenters of the "Bold Dragoon" looked upon "Miss Julia," as they called her, as a vastly-superior personage; but a few of the skippers, while pretending to regard her with feelings of reverence and awe, were often ungallant enough to try and make her ridiculous.

The landlady had one desire—a desire no one even guessed the strength of—namely, to make a good match. She knew her brother did not wish her to marry. He had often tried to demonstrate to her the wisdom of remaining single, and he had always held the threat over her head that he would evict and disinherit her if she married without consulting him and obtaining his consent.

M'Cormick's reason for not wishing that his sister should take a partner for life was chiefly because he felt certain she would marry a man who would be in some respects objectionable, and this would, he thought, serve to widen the breach existing between himself and his wife. Besides, he did not wish to see his hard-earned money squandered on some worthless member of society, and he was convinced his sister's choice would fall either on some good-looking ne'er-do-well, or on some plausible scoundrel, with perhaps a little money, who happened to be on the look-out for a comfortable home in his declining years.

It may be seen, therefore, that John M'Cormick's estimation of his step-sister's taste and judgment was not a very high one. Indeed there was no love lost between John M'Cormick and Julia Walsh. The former acted the part of protector towards the latter altogether from a sense of duty, and in respect for the memory of his mother, whose child Julia was.

During the afternoon of the fourteenth of March, some twenty years ago, M'Cormick had a short interview with his sister, which resembled the month of March in the manner of its proverbial beginning and ending. He had been in a particularly unpleasant mood on account of a serious quarrel with his wife—serious at least on his part, for Mrs M'Cormick always treated her husband with infinite scorn whenever, as was too often the case, he chose to pick a groundless quarrel with her.

"Look here, Julia!" he said abruptly to his sister, as they stood in the foreign skippers' room, "I know very well things won't go far wrong while I am in Sloughford and can keep my eye on you; but I have heard a few stories about

you lately, and if I find you carrying on with
any fellow without consulting me, you will find
yourself in the wrong boat, I can tell you. I
have always meant to act fairly by you. Don't
think your tossing your head makes any impression on me, madam! God knows I have done
my duty by you ever since my mother made
you over to me; but I'll stand no nonsense.
This place"—here he stamped his foot violently
on the floor, and struck the table a heavy blow
—"is mine—mine, I tell you. It may belong to
you one day if you don't go flying in my face,
but if you do, look out for squalls!"

"Indeed!" sneered Miss Julia, her bosom heaving
with a rage which she found herself powerless
to control. "I know well the cause of your
anxiety for my future welfare. It's all the nonsense that doll-faced chit, your wife, is putting
into your head."

"Chit!" cried M'Cormick furiously. "How dare
you! How dare you speak like that to me of
my wife! Get out of the house, woman. Get out
of *my* house! Do you hear me?"

Miss Walsh saw that she had made a false

move, and had angered her brother beyond measure. She therefore determined to be diplomatic, and burst into tears.

"Yes, I'll go. I'll leave the place," she sobbed. "I could not stand being treated by you as you have treated me now. You have been very good to me, and it breaks my heart to see you constantly viewing my actions in a wrong light." And she sank on a chair, and sobbed as if her heart would break.

M'Cormick's rough heart was touched by this spectacle of a broken-hearted woman—what man can resist a woman's tears?—and, his voice losing all its former harshness, he said,—

"Don't get on like that, Julia. I'm a madman when my cursed temper gets the better of me." He caught her hands and took them not ungently from her eyes. "There," he said, "forget it all. I know I'm a brute—but you don't know how it angers me to hear my wife spoken slightingly of."

"You must allow, John," whined Miss Walsh, "that it is very hard on me to have you constantly taxing me with carrying on flirtations instead of minding the business and making money—for that's what you mean, I know. I give you my word you wrong me."

"But why do you drag my 'wife's name into our disputes, Julia ? "

"Because I know she hates me. She looks upon me as the dirt beneath her feet," cried Miss Walsh, her temper for the moment getting the better of her discretion.

"Let me tell you that you are quite mistaken. I never heard Susan say one single word that could lead me to believe that she hated you. So far as I know, she never said anything against you in all her life."

"Said anything," sneered Miss Walsh, in an undertone ; "she's too cunning for that."

Fortunately her brother did not hear this remark. The mere thought of his wife had softened his wrath more effectually even than his sister's bogus tears, and had put him into a pleasant humour. His sister saw he had not overheard her hasty words, and determined to be more prudent.

M'Cormick was silent for a few minutes. Then

he said, " Well, Julia, I'll bid you good-bye now, for this will be an extra busy day. Don't think too badly of me. I have been a lot put out latterly over many things. Don't fret yourself about leaving this place. There is such a thing as a will, even if I were to die suddenly—but I mustn't say anything. I'll take care lawyers or bankers don't get hold of *my* will. I know a safer place not many hundred yards off from here. Good-bye, Julia; I sha'n't see you again before I sail."

Miss Walsh bade her brother a tender and tearful farewell, and saw him to the door.

Then she retired behind the counter, and seating herself before a small desk smoothed her hands and smiled complacently. She had learned one fact, at all events, which caused her to feel remarkably comfortable. Her brother had made his will. He had treated her handsomely in it; of that she was quite certain. He would not have hinted mysteriously at a will unless it were one by which she would be a gainer beyond her expectations. At the very least he had left her the " Bold Dragoon," and, no doubt, a lump of hard cash with it. She had been anxious that he should make his will, for a sailor's life is so uncertain—and she was quite under the impression that everything would go to her brother's wife if he died intestate.

Another fact she had got hold of, or almost got hold of, was that the will had been, or would be, left in charge of Mr Butler, the ship-broker. There was no one else in Sloughford whom her brother trusted implicitly. She would send for Butler's clerk, Madden. He was a communicative young fellow, and she had no doubt he was acquainted with all his employer's business secrets. Yes, Madden was the very person to aid her in discovering the nature of her brother's will. She would write a note to him asking him to call upon her the following evening, when her brother would have sailed from the port. She could never know an easy mind until the contents of the will were discovered.

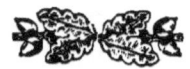

CHAPTER II.

GIVES A PEEP AT THE INTERIOR OF A SHIPBROKER'S OFFICE.

THE offices of James Butler, shipbroker, were situated on the quay, about a hundred yards lower down than the "Bold Dragoon." The house was an unpretentious one-storey building, with a rough-plastered front and a high red-tiled roof. It stood between a grocer's shop and a ship-chandler's. The former was a somewhat imposing-looking structure of three storeys, and the latter was about the same size as Butler's house, but offered a strong contrast to it by reason of a projecting eave, a bright yellow-washed front, and a slated roof.

Butler's father had been a shipbroker in Slough-ford, but late in life he had fallen in for a considerable sum of money and a small property in Devonshire. He had then left his native town and settled down in Ilfracombe. James Butler, who was an only son, had accompanied his father to Ilfracombe. He was then about twenty-two years of age. In less than ten years his father succeeded in frittering away his money and his property in mining speculations, and died penniless. His son had led a comparatively idle life during these years, occasionally renewing his acquaintance with Sloughford and its people.

When he was thirty-two years of age he returned abruptly to his native town, bringing with him a young girl, the only child of his dead sister. He took a private house of modest dimensions in Princes Street, and started as a ship-agent in his present office on the quay.

There were three shipbrokers in Sloughford at the time when this story opens. One confined himself exclusively to foreign or foreign-going ships; another, a retired sea-captain named Thornhill, divided with Butler, who was now in his forty-eighth year, the chief business of the port —the coasting ships' business. Butler occasionally dabbled in foreign waters, and he had an interest in a few of the smaller ships belonging to the port, for during the sixteen years he had been in business at Sloughford, he had been successful far beyond his expectations. He employed two clerks, Arthur Madden and Michael Ryan; and there was also attached to his establishment a messenger, or "runner," Edward Murphy — usually called Foxy Ned.

James Butler was a little above the medium height, and was somewhat sparely built. His clean-shaven face was pale and careworn. His eyes were dark and passionless in repose, but when he smiled a lambent flame illumined them. Those who knew Butler liked to see him smile. His clearly - cut features ordinarily bore an expression which was rather cold and repellant, but when he smiled, people felt they were in the presence of a man whose heart was full of kindliness and sympathy.

The shipbroker was on terms of that peculiar kind of familiarity which breeds not contempt, with all classes in his native town. Still his nearest friends were obliged to admit that there

was a strange, inexplicable reserve about him
which made them shy of prying into his affairs.
People wondered why he did not marry, but no
one cared to ask him why he preferred a single life.

Those who had business transactions with him
found they could place implicit trust in James
Butler. He was sharp-witted, unspeculative, and
straightforward. In Sloughford no one was held
in higher esteem, either by his equals in the
social scale, or by his inferiors, or superiors. His
superiors, or at least those who chose to fancy
themselves his superiors, were sometimes defer-
ential, always respectful, in his presence.

But whatever the inhabitants of Sloughford
thought of him, there was one class which almost
worshipped him—the coasting skippers—whether
natives of Sloughford or elsewhere, who had known
him for years, and who had come to look upon
him as the apotheosis of the shipbroker. Butler
did not seek, nor did he covet, anything bordering
on hero-worship. He was attached in a peculiar
way to his business, and to those by whose help
he had succeeded in making a comfortable pro-
vision for himself; and he treated all skippers,

whether young or old, rich or poor, in a fatherly
fashion; and they on their part were all eager to
prove themselves worthy of his regard.   Some of
his clients—not half-a-dozen, perhaps—he singled
out for his especial marks of friendship, and for a
few he could scarcely restrain his unexpressed contempt; but the majority was looked upon by him
in the same light as a good schoolmaster looks
upon his pupils; and he endeavoured to show that
" favouritism " had no place in his composition.

On the ground-floor of the shipbroker's office
there were two rooms, divided by a long, narrow
passage.   At one end of the passage was the
entrance door, and at the other end a door, usually
bolted, which opened on to a small yard where coals
and wood, for office use, and lumber, were scattered
in reckless confusion.

The private business of the place, such as the
correspondence and the consultations with mariners
or merchants, was conducted in the office at the left-
hand side of the passage.   Here also the business
of the foreign-going ships was transacted.   The
general office, where the coasting ships' business
was done, and where the coasting skippers sat, and

smoked, and chatted, read the newspapers, and signed their shipping documents, was at the right-hand side of the passage.

Butler was usually to be found in the office at the right-hand side, for he always seemed most happy when he was in the midst of a throng of merchant captains—arguing with them, advising them, adjusting their squabbles, listening to their good stories, or to their tales of trouble and hardship.

During the winter months there was always a roaring fire in this office, and there in the long evenings Butler, when the business of the day was well-nigh finished—after four o'clock the business proper of a shipbroker is virtually at an end for the day—he would take a chair and form one of the semi-circular group seated around the fireplace. He sat with his friends the skippers solely because it afforded him a harmless pleasure, and was oblivious to the fact that the skippers looked upon his presence in their midst as an act of condescending good-nature. When Butler was chatting with them they were as much delighted as a parcel of schoolboys playing leap-frog with their tutor.

It was amusing to watch the countenances and the actions of the skippers, when the shipbroker "took the chair." The mariner who, prior to Butler's approach, had arrogated to himself the poker, placed that fire-iron quietly and reverentially in a position where it might be easily grasped by the "governor." The mariner who had been carrying all before him by sheer weight of his trumpet-like voice, during a dispute as to the respective merits of Wellington and Napoleon, lowered his voice and said, "You'll put us all right, governor, won't you? You see, I have been trying to prove to the boys here that old Boncy really won the battle of Waterloo, and I'm blessed but they think 'tis daft I am. They'll take it from you though, governor, if you put it to them straight." "Excuse me, sir," another skipper would observe, rising and approaching the half-open door, "there's a nasty draught coming in there, right at your back." "This is a warmer corner of the fire, Mr Butler. Would you oblige by changing seats with me?" "I'll put a fresh shovelful of coals on the fire, sir, if you don't object."

And so on, each skipper vying with the other

to render the shipbroker as comfortable as possible.

During the evening of the fourteenth of March, Butler was seated at the fire at the general office —sometimes called Ryan's office, as Michael Ryan had his desk there—in the company of half-a-dozen mariners.

A drowsy silence had fallen upon the group. The worry of the day's business was over, and the shipbroker was indulging in a quiet nap. The skippers, fearful of disturbing him, had ceased to speak, and were now endeavouring—some of them in vain— to resist the soporific influence of the glowing fire.

We will take advantage of the silence, and introduce the skippers one by one.

That plump, bullet-head, little man with the twinkling blue eyes and the pasty complexion is Captain Patrick Carmody. His button-shaped nose looks like a bit of sealing wax stuck on a piece of whitey-brown paper. He wears no hair on his face except that bristly black tuft on his chin, which lends him a somewhat ferocious aspect. His countenance, it must be confessed, is a pretty fair index of his temperament, for he is extremely irritable.

One of his fellow-skippers has dubbed him "Carping Pat;" but the nickname is seldom mentioned in Carmody's hearing. He has a large family, and is sadly henpecked.

The low-sized, bow-legged man who wears the sou'-wester, and who is now sitting alongside Carmody, is Captain Anthony Arkwright. Though not a native of Sloughford, he is a well-known figure to young and old in that seaport. He is a master-mariner retired from business. He is fond of donning a sou'-wester on the smallest possible provocation—a threatening sky is sufficient excuse —in order that you may not forget that he has been a seaman, and is still at heart a seaman. For many years he has traded in and out of the port, and he has now settled down in Sloughford, having scraped together a very slender fortune— "a pittance," he terms it. He often hints mysteriously at "better days," and sometimes he makes mention of "a parent on the male side," who was connected largely with house property; but no one has ever discovered whether Arkwright senior was the owner of property, the agent, the architect, or one who carried a hod. He is exces-

sively fond of long words and uncommon phrases,
and with the aid of a powerful magnifying glass
—he is a trifle near-sighted—he studies Webster's
dictionary at every possible opportunity. His
friends try to refrain from laughing at his verbal
eccentricities, for he is too good-natured to be
made a butt of; but frequently he becomes a
most irritating companion. Usually he wears his
hands deep in his breeches pocket, and seldom
withdraws them except for the purpose of lighting a pipe, grasping a tumbler, or rubbing the
side of his nose nervously with his forefinger.
Now and again Captain Arkwright indulges too
freely in the wine of his adopted country; but
he is, after a fashion, a shrewd little man, and
he has the good taste, when he has drunk too
deeply, not to expose his condition to the mocking light of day. When he is overcome by pota-
tions, his mode of progression through the streets
of Sloughford—almost deserted after nightfall — is
peculiar. He does not, like the ignorant landsman, reel or stagger, but with the instinct of a
true-born tar, he makes "short tacks." When he is
desirous of turning a corner, he steadies himself

for a moment on one leg—a marvellous feat for a tipsy man—and suddenly (hiccuping " 'Bout ship!") wheels round the other leg; and then he continues to make further short tacks until necessity compels him to turn another corner. In this manner he generally continues to "beat a passage" safely to his own hall door. "Captain Arkwright on a wind" is a figure well remembered by old Sloughfordians.

That pale, hollow-cheeked, restless man with the bright red hair and the white fanatical forehead is Captain James Sullivan. He is slightly crazy about matters sanatorial: otherwise he is as dull and uninteresting a specimen of humanity as one could find in a seaport town. Sullivan is constantly discovering some wondrous and infallible means for restoring health and prolonging life. Nearly every voyage he changes his mind, and abandons one infallible nostrum for another still more infallible. He is not selfish or secretive; in fact, his most ardent desire is to benefit humanity at large by his marvellous discoveries.

The fat, heavily-built man, in the faded blue monkey-jacket, who is seated—his arms folded

across his broad chest—near Arkwright, is Captain
John Broaders. He has seen some fifty-five summers, but at first sight you would fancy he was
not more than forty years of age. His great round
cheeks almost shut out a view of his leaden-
coloured, expressionless eyes. His nose is broad
and flat, and his oily-looking face is hairless. It
is not easy to discover the line of demarcation
between his chin and his neck. It seems as if
Nature's plastic hand had been smoothed over
his features at an early period, and had rubbed
away all corners and squareness. He is not a
man of great conversational powers : his sentences
are usually brief ; but the end of every sentence
is punctuated with an impressive, self-satisfied
snort. Broaders is not given to levity, and
when he does condescend to smile, he tries to
convey the impression that he has conferred a
priceless boon upon you. When he walks through
the streets he holds his head high, and swings
his arms. He seldom stops to gaze about him,
but seems ever burdened with weighty business
cares. He drinks heavily, but he seldom loses
his physical or his mental balance, for his constitu-

tion is a powerful one. He has a theory that every man, as a matter of course, consumes as much ardent spirits as his constitution will stand. A moderate drinker he regards as a man in a poor state of health. A total abstainer in his eyes is one whose life is not worth a week's purchase.

The light-haired, full-bearded, delicate man, from whose countenance a foolish smile is seldom absent, is Captain Cummins. He is ten years younger than Broaders. Although he is narrow of chest and round of shoulders, he is outwardly a superior specimen of the coasting mariner. His black coat is fairly well cut, and his soft felt hat and snow - white shirt front help to contrast him favourably with the badly-dressed pair between whom he is now sitting—namely, Captains Sullivan and Broaders. Cummins has already buried two wives, and is eager to marry a third. He is aware that his smile is very fetching to feminine eyes, and his chiefest delight is to win a smile from ladies' eyes. He is indeed an arrant flirt; but there is a method in his amatory folly. He seldom makes downright love to any woman who is not possessed of attractions more substantial than

mere good looks. It is his intention to mate with
the landlady of some thriving public-house, and
then to retire from the sea, with all its dangers and
delights.

Standing at one side of the fireplace, his elbow
on the mantelpiece, his head supported by his
hand, is a wiry-looking, slovenly-dressed man with
small head and squarely-cut features. He is tall,
fully five feet eleven inches; slender of build, and
straight as a whip. A back view of him reminds
you of a colossal Dutch doll. His cast of countenance is severe—perhaps the scar across his cheek
has something to do with his severe aspect—
but his smile is a pleasant one. At present his
mental and physical energies are concentrated on
an effort to tickle surreptitiously Arkwright's
ear with a long straw. He appears to enjoy himself immensely at that worthy mariner's uneasiness
whenever he has succeeded in compelling him to
rub his ear; and it is not difficult to determine
that the big Dutch doll is fond of practical joking
in any shape or form. Indeed, Captain Tom
Bendall has the reputation of being the most in-
corrigible practical joker afloat. His pranks, it

must be added, are of a very mild quality ; but the business of the sea is so serious that a freak which to a landsman would seem to be very milk-and-waterish, would to a seafarer taste strongly of brine. Bendall enjoys his own jokes immensely, and he is subject to fits of chuckling which often threaten to induce convulsions.

Last, but not least, among the oddly-assorted group in the shipbroker's office, is that painfully well-dressed—for a seafarer—person who is now busy taking a reef in the string which secures his umbrella. This is Captain Augustine Flynn You may observe that he has a very solemn, nay funereal, cast of countenance, and that he is the only member of the group who wears a silk hat or carries an umbrella. He is called " the Bishop " by his companions, doubtless on account of his didatic discourse, his carefully-shaven face and well-washed hands, and his clean linen and silk hat—the mariners of Sloughford evidently considering his tastes and sympathies distinctively of an episcopal nature. He always speaks slowly and with earnestness, and he gives one the impression that he is addressing a congregation from

the pulpit. In his voice there is a peculiar and
mournful cadence which causes those who are "bad
sailors" to feel quite giddy. At one moment it
seems as if the Bishop were speaking from the
crest of the mounting wave and next moment as
if he had fallen headlong into the trough of the
sea, ay, to the very bottom of the ocean. He has
to endure a good deal of chaff from his nautical
friends, especially in connection with his silk hat
and umbrella. Bendall, however, is the only
skipper with whom Flynn ever cares to expos-
tulate. Although Captain Tom has a sincere
regard for the Bishop, he can never resist the
temptation of playing some childish pranks with
the "crozier," as he calls Flynn's umbrella, or
with the "mitre," as he calls the hat. Sometimes
it seems impossible to stave off a downright
quarrel between Captains Bendall and Flynn, but
coasting master-mariners of the old school were
peculiar in the matter of quarrels. They would
abuse each other in such a manner that a
stranger might reasonably imagine blows would
rapidly take the place of words; but somehow
they appeared to forget their ill-humour with

peculiar rapidity, and, instead of blows, hard words would be followed by remarkably soft speeches.

. . . .

The shipbroker and his friends were suddenly roused from their reveries by the entrance of Captain John M'Cormick, a big, raw-boned man with sad, stern, grey eyes.

" Good evening, governor. Good evening, lads," he smiled—not a pleasant smile by any means. " Enjoying yourselves, as usual ! "

It was easy to see that the master of the *Water Nymph* was in an excitable mood.

" Won't you sit down and join our little party ? " asked Butler, rubbing his eyes, wheeling round his chair, and facing the newcomer.

" No, governor. Not now, thank you. Much obliged all the same. I want to have a few words with you privately—you'll excuse me, skippers, won't you ? I know you'll all be thinking every minute an hour until the governor is back with you again. I won't keep him long, I promise you. Excuse me, won't you ? "

" Certainly, certainly," chorused the skippers, rising when the shipbroker rose.

"I am sorry," said the latter, "that you won't be sociable, M'Cormick, but if you want to say anything privately to me, you had best come into the other office. Madden is gone for the evening."

M'Cormick and Butler then left Ryan's office, crossed the passage, and entered the office at the other side—"Madden's office," as it was called.

The skippers re-seated themselves around the fire.

"Big Mac looks a bit scared," said Captain Cummins, when the door of Madden's office was closed.

"Oh! the usual complaint, no doubt. A row with the missus," sneered Captain Carmody. "The governor has always to be brought to Castle M'Cormick when Jack is after having a row with Jill."

"He's a rum customer is John M'Cormick," snorted Captain Broaders. "I often wonder the woman that's married to him doesn't cut and run. They say he bangs her about when he's in a temper."

"Believe half what you hear, neighbour," said Captain Bendall sententiously. "He's too fond of Mrs Mac for that sort of work, believe me."

"Quite a case of love in a cottage," laughed Captain Carmody derisively. "Woodbine Cottage, to wit."

"Fie, fie, Pat!" said the Bishop. "I wonder at you to be exhibiting such a carping, nasty manner. If a man doesn't happen to live peaceably and quietly with his wife, should that be made the subject of ribald jests in a public office ?"

But the skippers were wrong as to the cause of M'Cormick's visit.

When Butler closed the door of Madden's office behind himself and the master of the *Water Nymph*, he turned up the gas at full flare, and said,—

"Well, M'Cormick, what is troubling you now ?"

"I want you to do me a favour, Mr Butler. I hope you don't think I'm too great a trouble to you."

"Not at all, my dear sir. I am always happy to be of service to an old friend like yourself; but you mustn't ask me for a loan of a thousand pounds just now," he laughingly added. "Times are bad."

"Ah ! I'm glad to see you laugh, sir. I can't face

you when you are serious-looking. No! It isn't
money I want, though I don't forget long ago when
you did me many a good turn in that line. There
isn't a man like you, sir—"

"Surely," interrupted the shipbroker, "you didn't
come here to pay me compliments?"

"No, sir," replied M'Cormick sheepishly. "I want
you to take charge of some documents of importance
—of the greatest importance—to me. That's what
brings me here to-night."

"And why not place documents of importance with
a lawyer or a banker?"

"Because I don't want to—prying, blabbing lot!
There, excuse my temper, sir; but you know I'd
rather trust you than all the banks or lawyers in
Christendom; and when I take a crotchet into my
head, it isn't easy to drive it out."

"Yes, I am aware of that. All right, M'Cormick,
I'll lock your papers up, if that is what you want;
but I hope there is nothing of money value, for I
would not like the risk. This place could easily be
broken into, if a thief thought it worth his while to
break into it. As a rule, I don't keep money here at
night—more from habit than through fear, I must

admit—for I'm not over anxious to place temptation in anybody's way."

"There is nothing worth stealing, I assure you; the documents could not possibly be of the slightest use to anyone except myself."

"You're a strange man, M'Cormick. Come, what's the matter with you to-night? You look troubled. Out with it! By the way—you must excuse me for not asking you before—how is Mrs M'Cormick? Quite well, I hope?"

"Quite well, sir, thank you. I *am* troubled. I have been quarrelling with myself, and with her, and with everyone."

"I thought there was to be an end of that."

"Don't look so sternly at me, Mr Butler. Heaven knows I hate myself. I can't help my temper. It masters me—and she's as good as gold, sir, ten thousand times too good for a fellow like me. But she *won't* care for me, and it drives me wild sometimes when I think of it."

M'Cormick paused, and waited for a few minutes, hoping the shipbroker would say something; but Butler was silent.

"I made my will the other day, and although

I haven't been altogether bad to her in it, I haven't
been half good enough—and still I don't know.
Why should she, who hates me, despises me, have
my money? Sometimes I'm half-crazy, and think
of blowing out my brains, and leaving her without
a penny-piece."

"Sit down, M'Cormick. You are talking rubbish
now—pure rubbish. Have you been drinking?"

"No. Nothing to upset me."

"Well, sit down, man, and talk sense. Take
that stool. There, that's better. If your will is
a foolish or a vindictive one, burn it, burn it at
once, or get a new will drawn up before you
sail."

"No time for that now, even if I were so
inclined."

"Well, when you come back from Quebec. But
destroy the present will if you have treated your
wife unfairly in it."

"How would she be situated suppose I were to
die without a will?"

"Let me see," said the shipbroker, biting his
thumb; "she would, I think, get half of everything."

" And the other half ? "

" Would go to your sister. She is the only other relative you have."

" Damn her ! "

" For shame, M'Cormick ! It is shocking to hear you speak, as you sometimes do, of your sister."

" I am sorry for making use of coarse expressions before you, Mr Butler; but I don't look upon Julia as a sister at all ; and she made mischief in the beginning between my wife and myself. No, I won't destroy my will. I'll let it stand until I return. On the voyage I'll have time to think over everything."

M'Cormick, who was seated on a high stool at the office desk, now buried his face in his hands.

Butler, who had been standing with his back towards the fireplace, with a puzzled expression on his face, approached the master of the *Water Nymph*, and placing his hand on his shoulder, said gently,—

" Look here, John M'Cormick; you know I have a sincere regard for you. Why can't you turn over a new leaf ? Quick-tempered as you are, there is only one point on which you are utterly unreasonable."

"My wife!" said M'Cormick, lifting his head. "Why, can't she see I'd give my eyes for a word or a token of affection from her!" and he dashed his hand roughly across his face.

"Be a man, M'Cormick!" said the shipbroker tenderly; "you are to blame, not she. No woman would stand your absurd outbursts of temper. Instead of treating your wife kindly aud gently in the beginning, you thought fit to show yourself in your worst light to her. You abused her, bullied her, and sulked, because she couldn't see a young Adonis in you. And now you are surprised she has not learnt to love you."

"She hates and despises me."

"Nonsense. You know better; and if she did, you have only yourself to blame. Remember I implored you, when you asked my advice, not to make Susan Neville marry you. I knew there was little likelihood of your living happily together. There was the difference in ages for one thing; and then you ought to have reflected that, while you were brought up and lived the best part of your life among the roughest of the rough, she was reared in the midst of refinement.

"Curse refinement!"

"Ay, that was what you always said; but what is the good arguing or lecturing? What's done can't be undone; and if you would only determine even now, earnestly determine, to win your wife's regard by kindness, I am confident you would succeed."

"I don't believe it. But, Mr Butler, I'm taking up your time."

M'Cormick got off the stool and placed his hand in the breast-pocket of a capacious overcoat.

"I'll leave this case in your hands, sir, and I'll ask you to give me your word you'll tell nobody about it or about our conversation to-night."

"Yes, I will give you my word."

M'Cormick handed the shipbroker a tin case fastened with a small padlock. Butler took his keys from his pocket and opened the heavy door of the office safe.

"Will it be all right there?" inquired M'Cormick.

"Certainly. No one except Madden has a duplicate of the key of the safe door, and no one except myself has the key of this inside drawer where you see me now placing your case. I suppose the will is here?" tapping the case as he placed it in the inside of the safe.

"Yes, sir. I didn't mean to tell you about my will when I came in, but it slipped on me somehow. I didn't want anyone to know about it; but after all I suppose it's only so much waste paper, for I'll make up my mind to alter it and leave her everything. I feel better since I had a talk with you. I always feel better after a talk with you. I'm sorry now I'm going to sail to-morrow."

"I wish you had left the documents with your lawyer, or at the bank, for I have responsibilities enough without this," said Butler, closing the door of the safe. "I do hope you have put nothing of money value into the case. Someone may hear—it may slip from yourself, for your tongue often runs away with you—that you have been depositing papers of value with me, and as I told you, I can give you no guarantee of the security of an office like this."

"Don't have the slightest uneasiness, sir. No one knows the object of my visit here, and no one will know of it from me. Besides, as I have already assured you, I am asking you to take charge of nothing which could be of the smallest value to anybody. But won't you promise me to be silent about it—about everything that passed between us to-night?" asked M'Cormick, his hand on the handle of the office door.

"I never break my word, whatever it may cost me," said the shipbroker, turning down the gas.

CHAPTER III.

CONTAINS SOME IDLE CONVERSATION.

THE following day the barque *Water Nymph*, six hundred and seventy tons register, lay at anchor in the river Slough, ready to proceed to sea. The wind was from the east; and as the *Water Nymph* was notoriously a fast sailer, and her commander and sole owner notoriously a "driver," it was expected, should the easterly wind last, that the barque would arrive at her port of destination, Quebec, in less than three weeks.

A group of coasting skippers—the same group which had congregated in Butler's office the previous evening—stood on the quay of that seaport, and shook their heads ominously when they saw the tug-boat paddling towards the barque about eleven o'clock in the forenoon.

The day was dull. Overhead, ragged gloomy-looking patches of cloud were borne swiftly across the sky; the air was raw and biting; and the river, a muddy-green mass of water, was swollen and angry-looking. The shrill melancholy cry of the seagull was heard high above every other sound which reached the quay. No wonder then that the Sloughford skippers were not in high spirits, and that they were little inclined for conversation, as they stood gazing at the black restless hull of the barque.

Captain Carmody was the first to break the silence.

" Mark my words, boys," he cried, turning round and addressing the group, " the *Water Nymph* will get a peppering in the Western Ocean this trip."

" It's a toss-up between the ice and the equinoctials," said Bendall, hastily taking a straw from Arkwright's ear and putting his hand behind his back ; " but I'm game to lay odds on the ice. What say you, neighbour Arkwright ? "

" Too anticipatory by a calendar month is my

ultimatum," said Arkwright, scratching his ear. "Big Jack's impetuosity will, as you suggest, Captain Bendall, eventuate in his annihilation."

"The barque isn't as young as she used to be," said Sullivan. "There's no hiding the fact that we all grow older as the years go by, and still we neglect to set up a stock of health for our old age. Now, perhaps I haven't told you, neighbours, I've just discovered that salt in large quantities—"

"Oh, man, dear," interrupted Carmody, "for the love of goodness will you not be bothering us with yourself and your nostrums. 'Tis fairly persecuted we are between your crazes and Arkwright's jawbreakers."

Having silenced Captain Sullivan, Carmody lifted one hand to his forehead, and shading his eyes, cried,—

"There they go at the anchors, boys; and, if I'm not very much mistaken, that's Mrs M'Cormick herself that's being rowed ashore in the boat. Well," taking down his hand and staring fiercely at his companions, as if one or all of them had seriously offended him, "I only hope big Jack won't fall foul of an iceberg, and make a widow of the decent woman."

"That oughtn't to cause her a great deal of grief," snorted Broaders.

"Better say that to M'Cormick himself, John," rejoined Captain Martin Cummins. "He'd make a widow of your missus pretty quick, John, if he heard you talking like that."

"Well," said Captain Arkwright, "I would not cast imputations against the lady if she didn't lament herself into a sarcophagus after her husband, supposing he was to collide with an iceberg, for he's got the most extremely heinous temper—"

"What are you saying, man? What ails you at all? What sort of things are them sarphocasuses you are getting into your head this time?" asked Carmody. "You ought to have one of them shoved down your gullet. I hate to hear a man talking like you, Arkwright, at your time of life, too. I wish you'd learn sense, man."

Arkwright laughed scornfully, but said nothing.

"Ah, she's a nice, beautiful woman," sighed Cummins softly, as if he were awaking from a pleasant dream. "Not," he added, quickly and

nervously, "that I wish Jack M'Cormick any mis-
hap, all the same."

"What on earth are you driving at, Cummins?"
asked Bendall.

An angry look stole into Cummins' eyes, but he
made no reply to his tormentor.

"What is it you're driving at, Cummins?"
again demanded Captain Tom. "I'm blest if I
don't think you were dreaming already of making
love to big Mac's widow. Oh, dear! oh, dear!
what is the world coming to at all?"

"Mind your own business, Tom Bendall!"
snarled Cummins. "You have a deal of impudence
to be meddling in what doesn't concern you; and
I'd have you to know—"

"Fie! fie! gentlemen," interrupted Captain Flynn,
"I must speak at last, for I am fairly shocked
at your conversation. You have no right—I address myself to you all—to talk in this light
and frivolous manner of any man's wife; and it
ill becomes you, Tom Bendall, to be laughing
and joking about making love to widows that
are far, let us hope and pray"—here he lifted
his eyes reverently and made a sweeping gesture

with his left hand, a wonderfully small, well-formed hand for a seafarer—"far, I repeat, from being widows yet. Fie, fie, fie! And you too, Pat," addressing Carmody; "for I think it was you that began this light and dangerous conversation into which most of you have drifted as it were into a whirl-pool. Oh, fie, fie! to let your tongues scandalise you!"

"Hear, hear!" cried Arkwright excitedly, with-drawing his hands from his pocket; and rubbing his nose violently, he made a mental note to look up the word "scandalise." He knew all about "scandalised mainsails," but "scandalised tongues" puzzled him.

"Bravo Bishop! Let 'em have it hot and strong," cried Captain Carmody, almost at the same moment that Arkwright spoke. Then shading his eyes again with his hand, he continued, in a rasp-ing tone,—"There's no mistake about it. That *is* Mrs Mac herself in the boat. Doesn't see enough of the dear man ashore, I suppose. Well, wonders will never cease. What a pair of turtle-doves her-self and Jack have turned themselves into! Well, I'm blessed!"

"It would be a merciful dispensation of Provi-

dence, sir, if you were!" exclaimed Arkwright indignantly. "And what business have you, pray, to
sneer at anybody? Faugh! If there's one thing I
despise more than another it is innuendo."

"In-new what?" asked Carmody, with rising
temper.

"Shame, shame, gentlemen!" groaned the Bishop.
"I don't see what right any of you have to take
it for granted that John M'Cormick and his wife
are not a united pair."

"The Lion and the Unicorn!" laughed Carmody
mockingly.

Owing to a lifelong study of the Royal Arms on
the doors of various Custom Houses, he had arrived
at the belief that these animals were emblematic of
a loving and undying partnership.

"Ah," murmured the Bishop dreamily, "I remember her well before John M'Cormick forced her into
matrimony with himself."

"Forced her!" exclaimed Arkwright; "then you
mean to impute that she did not marry of her
own free will. You know," he added apologetically, "I am not as much at home about the his-
tories of our worthy townfolk as the rest of you,

being partly an alien by birth. What is her story, Captain Flynn? I do not inquire through motives of ignorant curiosity, but merely for wholesome information."

"You see," said the Bishop, who was ever eager for a quiet gossip, "she was engaged to a young fellow belonging to the town, a son of a wealthy merchant, Dalton by name."

"I remember him. Rather a reckless sort of man. Shot himself, didn't he?"

"No. He died suddenly, nevertheless; and—I know how matters have got mixed in your head—ruin was the result, not only to his family, but to others, for his death was the cause of dragging down the present Mrs M'Cormick's father, and *he* shot himself. Now do you see where you got hold of the wrong end of the yarn?"

"I do. I do. Thing's *will* get blended promiscuously in a man's mind. Well?"

"The Nevilles—that's Mrs M'Cormick's people—were ruined; the Daltons—the young man's name was Richard Dalton—were ruined.

"Yes, yes. I apprehend. He is at sea now, this Richard Dalton—master of a ship, is he not?"

" He is. A nice, agreeable young man, too, as far as my recollection goes. Well, the widow—Mrs Neville, I mean—got to the end of the tether—a clean-swept hold, if I may so remark it—a couple of years after her husband's untimely death—for there was something saved out of the wreck to keep her going—and then John M'Cormick, attracted by the beauty of his present lady, proposed, and her mother forced her to accept him, to save the family."

" Mrs Neville is not alive at present, is she ? "

" No. She did not live long after the marriage of her daughter. Poor lady ! I fear she is not over happy."

" Mrs Neville ? "

" No, the daughter."

" M'Cormick, I should say, was a most uncongenial man."

" Most uncongenial," echoed the Bishop, who had himself a *penchant* for odd words and absurd phrases.

" Well, Anthony," said Carmody, " have yourself and the Bishop got the lockjaw yet? Come, boys," addressing his companions, " who'll stand drinks round at the 'Nest ?' We may as well wish a prosperous voyage to the *Water Nymph*, and wash your tongues clean at the same time."

"I don't mind if I stand," said Bendall, "although there's a big crowd of you here — but hang the expense! It will all come out of the main hatch."

"Tom, you are a queer fellow," smiled Captain Cummins.

"There she goes!" snorted Broaders, pointing to the *Water Nymph*. "Let's give Big Jack a parting salute."

The skippers took off their hats, and waving them, shouted "Safe voyage!"

"I wonder Mac isn't on the poop to return our salute," said Cummins. "Well, I wish him no harm, I'm sure, even though he has no manners."

"I'll take odds he eats his Easter Sunday dinner in Quebec," said Captain Bendall, "for I admire his pluck. But up anchor, my bullies! the sun is over the mainyard, and it's time to wet our whistles."

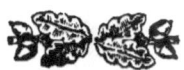

CHAPTER IV.

A SAILOR'S WIFE.

WHEN the skippers on the quay had begun to discuss M'Cormick's affairs, domestic and maritime, Mrs M'Cormick was seated alone in the cabin of the *Water Nymph*. A black cashmere dress enveloped her slight, graceful figure. The broad collar of creamy lace round her neck, and the lace cuffs at her wrists, challenged attention to the whiteness of her throat and hands. A heavy mantle lay on the seat alongside her, and her hat and gloves were on the cabin table. She wore no jewellery—neither bracelet, brooch, nor earrings—and on her slender finger there was but one ring—the wedding ring.

As Mrs M'Cormick sat at the cabin table, one hand supporting her chin, her thoughts flew back

to the time when she had been a little girl. The
tears sprang to her eyes as she called to mind
her father, whom she loved, and whose idol she
was—her reckless, handsome father, whose large
dark eyes and a little of whose spirit she in-
herited. Her memories of her mother were not so
pleasurably sad, for her mother had always been
cold and selfish. How strange was the contrast
between the refinement of her father's home and
surroundings, and the coarseness of her present circumstances! She was growing impatient at the
delay. Why had her husband, knowing how she
hated the ship, sent for her this morning? And
the constant tramp, tramp of the heavy-booted
sailors overhead. How it irritated her!

The sound of footsteps descending the cabin
stairs changed the current of her thoughts.

"Well, Susan," said Captain M'Cormick, seating
himself near his wife and picking up one of her
gloves. "I hope I haven't worn your patience out
altogether. There's always something wrong at
the last moment when a ship wants to get to sea.
Look here, Susan," he continued abruptly, after a
short awkward pause, "why can't you try to care a

little bit for me ? You needn't smile. I'm serious.
You know," he went on hurriedly, "I'd give my eyes
to feel you loved me. I own I'm not good enough
for you—anyone need only look at the pair of us
to tell that you're miles above me; but—but, you
might show a little bit of affection towards me
sometimes. Don't look so frightened, child. Here
we are nearly seven years man and wife, and I
have never said half as much to you since the
week we were married."

M'Cormick spoke with a strange tremor in his
rough voice. His wife was still silent. She did
not know what to say. She felt confused and
dazed by her husband's unexpected words.

"I know I am not what people call a good husband," continued M'Cormick, after another awkward
pause, "but can you blame me altogether ? " You
drove me wild with your coldness and your haughti-
ness. And when I found you could not or would
not care for me, you made my wretched temper
forty thousand times worse than ever."

" I ! "

" Yes. I don't want to blame you. I suppose
you had no wish to do so. But can you blame

me, I ask you again ? I haven't been a bad husband in some respects, at any rate. I have never
stinted you about money. Have I ? "

He spoke fiercely, and the glove which he had
been twisting round his fingers was now torn
down the middle.

"I never said you did, John," replied Mrs M'Cormick, in a tremulous tone. Her husband's vehemence
frightened her, and she scarcely knew what she was
saying. "Indeed, indeed, you have been very kind
and considerate to me in many ways. But surely,"
she continued, recovering herself and looking up into
M'Cormick's face, "you did not expect to find a
love-sick wife in me. I told you," she continued,
with the faintest of smiles, "I had no heart, and
you declared you were perfectly content to take
me without a heart."

"I was a liar!" exclaimed M'Cormick gruffly
—"but there, don't let us say any more about
it. It's no use, no use." And leaning forward
on the cabin table, he buried his face in his
hands.

Susan M'Cormick did not consider she was un-
truthful when she declared she was heartless, so

far, at least, as her husband was concerned. She
believed her heart had died within her the day
she had written her last letter to Dick Dalton. But
something in M'Cormick's voice touched her; some
new chord seemed to vibrate within her. Had she
been just to the man with whom, however unwill-
ingly, she had cast her lot? Was it right that
she should have made no effort to render him less
miserable? for, almost for the first time, it struck
her how profoundly miserable her husband was.
What right had she, after all, to be cold to him
whom she had vowed, falsely vowed, no doubt, to
love, honour, and obey? Had duty no claim upon
her? Would it not have been far better to have
bowed to circumstances, and to have made up her
mind to be a dutiful wife, and at least show some
tokens of affectionate regard to the man beside her?
Might not she herself—were she to look upon the
matter in a purely selfish light—have been infinitely
happier had she done so? Was caste everything?
Could not the human heart bridge over seemingly
impassable gulfs of social distinction? She never
doubted that her intelligence was far superior to her
husband's, that her sympathies and tastes were widely

different from his, but was this a justifiable plea for her own conduct ?

These thoughts passed rapidly, and perhaps vaguely, through her mind, and she almost felt her heart go out to the rough, ungainly-looking man who sat close beside her with bowed head. She was on the point of saying something tender to him.

Raising his head, and gazing sadly at his wife, M'Cormick instinctively felt that some great unhoped-for change was coming over her, and with a quick, glad cry, he put his arm round her waist.

She freed herself instantly. She was not yet prepared for love-making.

" Come," said M'Cormick, with a trace of temper. " I have a right to place my arm round you if I like, Am I so hateful that my touch disgusts you ? Oh ! I'm sick of it, sick of it !" he exclaimed, standing up and moving away from the table.

" John, John," cried Mrs M'Cormick, affected by the despairing tone of his voice, " don't be so down-hearted, like a good fellow. Sit down again. Do sit down. You are the nearest in the world to me now, and although I did not marry you of my own free will, and although we have not got on very well

together, I would be very, very sorry to fret you.
If you will only believe me, I like you better than
anyone else in the world now. There, won't that
satisfy you ?"

She smiled, and her husband again seated himself
at her side. His compressed lips trembled visibly.
He silently stretched out his hand, and clasped his
wife's hand.

For a few minutes there was silence in the cabin ;
husband and wife sat with bowed heads, each
anxious to break the silence, neither knowing how
to break it. At last Mrs M'Cormick, lifting her
head, spoke,—

"You told me this morning that you were anxious
to see me on some business matter before you sailed."

"Yes," he replied, a little wearily. "I wanted to
say a few words to you. I have been worried and
troubled a good deal; perhaps that is some excuse
to offer for my surliness lately. The fact is," he
continued with more energy, "I have made my
will."

"Made your will. Surely that could not have
caused you trouble."

"It has—it does. It has troubled me a good deal

since I made it, because I haven't treated you fairly.
I should at anyrate have consulted you, Susan;
but I was out of sorts as usual. However, I promise
you it won't be my last will. I feel a changed man
since last night."

" And is that your only trouble now—I mean
about your will ? "

" No. I have had all sorts of strange presentiments latterly."

" You indulging in presentiments ? About what,
pray ? "

" Death ! "

" Oh, nonsense, John ! " cried his wife, with an
involuntary shudder; " you never looked in better
health."

" Health hasn't much to do with it. I have had
horrible dreams about drowning."

" Probably the result of late suppers."

" You *will* make fun of it, I see; but you don't
know how strongly the impression has got hold of
me that I sha'n't make many more voyages."

" Why make one more, then ? You told me long
ago you could easily afford to give up the sea."

" And would you be contented," asked M'Cormick

eagerly, " if I did ? I am afraid you see a great deal too much of me as it is."

" Why do you think so badly of me ? " she asked, with a mixture of tenderness and petulance. " By all means give up the sea, if I am the only stumbling-block. I have no fancy for it any more than your-self. I hate the sea."

" Ay ! " interrupted her husband, shaking his head ; " and, I fear, those who live by it."

" You wrong me again. Stop ashore by all means. Believe me, I am asking you to do so from my heart. Let us go away somewhere, anywhere. I begin to detest Sloughford. There, forgive my hastiness. Sometimes memories of the old town make me sad beyond measure. I don't hate it ; I love it. But won't you give up the sea, John ? "

" I will, I will. I would have done so long ago, but I feared you would run away from me, or do something desperate," he smiled, " if I were to be always at your side. Oh, Susan ! you don't know what a load you have lifted from me. God bless you, old girl. I'll look for a master for the *Water Nymph* at once—I mean," he went on, after a momentary pause, his thoughts rapidly changing from his wife to his other love, his ship—"after the year is out. I'm bent on making three North American voyages this season."

"Why not get someone else to make them for you?"

"Oh, that would never do, Susan," he laughed. "I must see the year out. I must make those three voyages myself. I'm bent on it."

"You are a strange man. A few moments ago you were complaining of presentiments of drowning —I may tell you I don't attach the slightest importance to presentiments of any sort—but if my mind were troubled about the sea, and if I were in your position, I'd very soon bid good-bye to the best ship afloat."

"Ah! Susan, you were never cut out for a sailor's wife." Mrs M'Cormick smiled faintly. "You don't know the anxiety a sailor feels to make a good finish. I'll give up the sea with a contented mind if I can carry three cargoes of deals to Sloughford this season, for that won't be a bad year's work, I I can inform you, and it will help to make things more comfortable for us. It will give the old craft a good name, and she'll sell all the better. But about the will, old girl."

"What about it?" She spoke a little sharply. Somehow the term "old girl" grated harshly on her ears, notwithstanding all her good resolutions.

"Now that I come to think of it, I ought not to say anything about it, for I promised Butler I wouldn't. The will is in his charge. You must not let anyone know I have told you of it. After all, it is only so much waste-paper. Don't think I am growing crazy yet, but my memory seems all rickety lately. My real anxiety was to tell you not to think I was going to act badly by you, should you by any chance come to hear from Butler that I had made a will without consulting you. I'd have altered the whole thing this morning if I had time to go ashore, for I mean you to have everything, everything, Susan. I hate myself —God knows I do—for having ever said a harsh word to you."

M'Cormick was about to fling his arms around his wife's neck, when a loud voice from the cabin stairs startled him.

"Just on the high water, skipper. Excuse me for interrupting you, sir; but she'll be tending if we don't get the anchors up at once."

" All right, Mr Mate," cried M'Cormick.

Then standing up, he turned to his wife and said hurriedly,—

" We must get on deck, Susan."

Mrs M'Cormick rose, and her husband took up her mantle.

" Won't you forgive me ? " he asked, helping her with her mantle. " That Manx man in the tug will be swearing his head off if I don't make a start at once. I'll write to you from Quebec. Good-bye, my dearest old girl," he cried, seizing her hands and kissing her. " At all events we part good friends, don't we, if nothing more ? "

" Something more, I hope," replied his wife. " I feel now how badly I have behaved towards you —but let us say no more about it," pressing his hand. " Let our actions in the future prove we are in earnest."

" Agreed ! " he cried joyously. " Now, good-bye once more."

And, with a lighter heart than he had known for many a day, the captain of the *Water Nymph* led the way up the cabin staircase.

CHAPTER V.

DISCUSSES THE AFFAIRS OF THE SHIPBROKER'S CLERK.

ARTHUR MADDEN was not a native of Sloughford, and of his early history the Sloughfordians knew little or nothing. He had appeared one morning, about ten years prior to the sailing of the *Water Nymph*, at his desk in Butler's office. Nobody seemed to know where or how the shipbroker had picked up his new clerk, and nobody cared to catechise Butler.

Madden's account of himself was simple. He had been born and brought up in Swansea. His parents had died while he was quite a child, and some friends had sent him to school. When he had left school he had been placed in the office of a Swansea shipbroker, and his coming to Sloughford was due to the appearance of an advertisement in a

Swansea newspaper. Butler had advertised for a clerk who could speak French and Italian, and he had applied for the situation.

He was still at the sunny side of thirty; but he was stout enough to be described as corpulent. His hair was dark and closely cropped, and a long black moustache covered his upper lip. The expression of his features in repose was inanimate and passionless; but when he smiled his cold blue eye grew bright and lit up his face. His lips as he smiled would part widely, disclosing a set of white even teeth. His nostrils would become visibly distended, and the lines round his cheeks deeply furrowed. Some reckoned him a good-looking man; others went so far as to term him positively handsome.

Madden possessed a temper which it seemed impossible to ruffle. He was loud of voice, boisterous even; and his laugh was contagious. He was popular in Sloughford, yet he could not boast of having many friends. He had no respect for youth or age, rich or poor; and he would sacrifice anything for the sake of a joke. He looked upon women in general as a somewhat inferior class of beings. As a rule he did not seek the society of the softer sex, but he was always ready and willing to make love; and as he was never in earnest, he usually succeeded in winning the affections of those whom he singled out for conquest. Love-making with him was a harmless pastime, and it was useless to suggest to him that there was a serious side to the matter. Among his many conquests he could reckon that of Maggie Ryan, the sister of his fellow-clerk, Michael Ryan. Maggie, a pale, delicate girl, some eight or ten years Madden's junior, looked upon herself as his future wife, and the knowledge of this conviction of hers was a source of serious mental trouble to the young man. Maggie was the only girl of his acquaintance whose hopes and disappointments ever cost him a thought. He was well aware she was deeply in love with him, and to the best of his ability, he simulated a deep affection for her. He felt her sensitive nature would receive an ugly shock if he were to throw her over. "I may change my mind one of these days," he sometimes mused, "and become a marrying man. After all, Maggie is positively a nice-looking girl. She is awfully in love with me, and we might get on very well together. I know I ought to be more candid with her; but it would quite upset her if I were to break away from her altogether. Poor little girl! How stupid women are!" Usually his musings ended in a laugh, as he conjured up pictures of himself hampered with the cares of married life.

Michael Ryan, whose affection for his sister was deep and unbounded, was pained beyond measure at Madden's frivolous conduct with regard to Maggie, but Michael was too mild-spirited to remonstrate with his fellow-clerk. Madden played the part of small tyrant over Ryan, not because his nature was a tyrannical one, but he had an ever-present desire to ward off anything that might worry him, and he felt that Ryan would, if he only got the opportunity, take him to task about his conduct towards Maggie.

When he received Miss Walsh's message the morning the *Water Nymph* sailed from Sloughford, he was a little puzzled to imagine what the landlady could require him for. At first he supposed she wished him to aid her in recovering some debt which one of Butler's many clients owed her; but Miss Walsh had contrived to sur-

round her letter with such a halo of mystery that
he concluded it was something of a different nature
from commonplace debt - collecting which was at
the bottom of the invitation to the "Bold Dragoon."

He had no knowledge of the existence of M'Cormick's will; but when Miss Walsh told him that,
in her opinion, the document was in Butler's possession, Madden felt he was in duty bound to
declare he knew all about it, and that it would
be a comparatively easy matter for him to give
the landlady the information she required. Of
course, he assured her, he would take care that
everything would be kept strictly secret.

His intention was to play some practical joke
on Miss Walsh, but at the moment he could not
decide what the nature of the joke ought to be.
To assure her, after a decent interval had elapsed,
that she had been left everything by her half-
brother, and that the master of the *Water Nymph*
was a millionaire, would probably result in some
piece of extravagant conduct on the part of the
landlady, and in Madden's eyes nature had destined
her exclusively as a subject for sound practical
joking.

After leaving the "Bold Dragoon" he walked down the quay, and it suddenly occurred to him that something profitable to himself might be made out of M'Cormick's will. He readily believed it was to be found in Butler's possession; and if he could gain any advantage by ascertaining how M'Cormick had devised his property, he saw no reason why he should not gain that advantage, and many reasons why he should. He would endeavour to think out some plan for getting a peep at the will, and afterwards he could make up his mind whether he would confine himself to playing the fool with Miss Walsh, or not. If Butler had the document, his niece might, possibly, be able to give him some information about it. If it lay in the office safe there could be little difficulty in placing his hands upon it. Yes, he would try to discover if Miss Cadogan knew anything.

He was a constant visitor at the shipbroker's house, and Helen always seem pleased to see him.

"By George!" he cried, forgetting for the moment M'Cormick and everything connected with him, "what an ass I have been! There is one of the handsomest girls in the town, and I have never even thought of making love to her. She is young, and I suppose the governor will leave everything to her; so I may call her wealthy. She is lively, and always in good humour—in fact, the one girl in Sloughford that would suit me exactly. How stupid of me never to have thought of her before. Well, I'll make up for lost time this evening, if I only get a chance. There's nothing like going straight to the point with women."

He hastily turned up a side street, and in a few minutes the hall door of Butler's hospitable house had closed behind him. Madden, to his intense delight, found Miss Cadogan alone in the drawing-room.

"Your uncle is out, I am told," he said, shaking hands with Butler's niece.

"Yes," she said. "He has gone to see a friend this evening. Won't you sit down?"

"Thank you."

"I don't think uncle will be long away. Have you anything to say to him? or can I do anything for you?"

"Oh, nothing particular. The fact is, I thought I would call, as I happened to be in Princes Street."

"We don't often see you here. Uncle is always pleased when you do happen to call."

"It is awfully good of him. I wonder he can bear the sight of me after office hours; but, Miss Cadogan," lowering his voice, and imparting into his words all the tenderness he could command, "much as it gratifies me to know that the governor takes an interest in me, there is one other thing you could, if you liked, tell me, which would give me even greater pleasure."

M'Cormick's will had again vanished from his thoughts.

"What is that, Mr Madden?" asked Helen, her cheeks colouring.

"Well," stammered Madden, who now found he was unable, easily as love-making came to him, to plunge *in medias res* as rapidly as he could desire. "Might I ask you a very pointed question?"

"Really, I can't imagine what you mean by a pointed question," said Helen, standing up.

"Miss Cadogan, one moment! I am sure you will answer me—are *you* pleased when I call— I should say, are my visits here objectionable to you?"

"Objectionable! Why should they be? What a strange question to ask?"

"Perhaps I do not put the matter in the right way. I mean—I mean—do you wish me to— Oh, you must surely guess what I mean," he cried, his face growing crimson from embarrassment.

"Really, I do not understand you, Mr Madden."

"Miss Cadogan!" cried Madden, rising, and seizing her hand, which she quickly drew away, "need I say I have a sincere, a most sincere regard for you?"

It struck him there was something absurd in this observation, so he thought it would be best now to make one supreme effort, and have the worst of it over.

"You know—you must know—that I love you."

"Are you endeavouring to amuse yourself at my expense, Mr Madden?" she asked indignantly.

"Amuse myself!' he cried. "Is it likely? It

is not a thing to treat as a joke. I am quite in earnest, Miss Cadogan. I do wish you to believe I am quite in earnest. Pray believe me. It is a matter which will decide my future happiness or misery."

"Really! I have always looked upon you as a gentleman incapable of being serious about anything. Please do not indulge in this sort of fun in my presence, or you will compel me to speak to my uncle about it."

"Oh, it is too bad. It is positively too bad," he cried. "Miss Cadogan, what do you take me for? Do you really and truly believe I would make a jest of a matter so sacred?" Then, with an air of mingled resignation and despair, he murmured,—"I am sorry if I have said anything to displease or offend you. It was unwise, perhaps, to have spoken so abruptly; but the promptings of my heart carried me away. I could not help myself. But I beg, I pray, you will believe man was never more earnest than I am. I had no right, I own, to take advantage of your uncle's absence this evening; but Mr Butler has always been so kind and generous to me that I thought he might possibly not object to my paying my addresses to his niece. Good-bye, Miss Cadogan," mournfully, " I can only regret you will not believe in the sincerity of my declaration."

Helen could scarcely believe he was in earnest. For years she had been accustomed to meet Madden, but she had never for a moment dreamt of regarding him in any other light than that of an ordinary acquaintance. She had always been glad to see him, for Madden's unfailing high spirits always enlivened her uncle, and her uncle's happiness occupied the first place in her thoughts. She scarcely knew now whether she ought to be seriously offended or whether she ought to be gratified, or whether she ought to insist upon regarding Madden's declaration of love as a dangerous kind of joke. The declaration had been so abrupt and unexpected that she was confused, and knew not what to think or what to say. However, she felt it was best to put an end to the present embarrassment at once. Extending her hand, she said,—

" Good-bye, Mr Madden. I am sorry if I have really wounded your feelings."

Madden was now standing near the door, and

was quite as anxious as Helen to put an end to the interview.

"Good-bye, Miss Cadogan," taking her hand and raising it to his lips. "Perhaps ere we meet again you will have learned to think less badly of me."

She made no answer, but stood with her bent head and crimson cheeks as he bowed and made a hasty exit.

CHAPTER VI.

THE SKIPPERS' SYMPOSIUM.

THERE was a gathering of the clans in the "Bold Dragoon." All the skippers who had been watching the departure of the *Water Nymph* earlier in the day, with the exception of Captain Augustine Flynn, lounged into the Nest while Madden was engaged in conversation with Miss Walsh.

Every man, as he seated himself round the fireplace, gripped his trousers above the bend of the knee, and with a couple of jerks drew the end of the trousers leg about three inches above his boots. Captain Arkwright, who always wore shoes, exposed four or five inches of sock. The unwritten law evidently regulated the sock exposure at three inches, but Captain Arkwright's words and deeds were generally in inverse proportion to his stature.

For nearly an hour the skippers sat almost in silence. All were drinking very slowly: some were smoking; and occasionally one of the mariners would close his eyes and fall quickly asleep.

"I wonder," snorted Captain Broaders, about eight o'clock, "Augy Flynn hasn't turned up. He told me he would join us this evening. Look here, Bendall, you must let the man alone. I know it's your fault he fights so shy of us lately."

Bendall, who was leaning forward, his elbows on his knees, and his hands supporting his head, sat upright in his chair, and was about to reply to Broaders, when Carmody's shrill voice vibrated through the room:

"In the name of Heaven! what's that you are doing, Captain Sullivan?"

Sullivan was holding a lump of salt over his glass of grog, and was crushing the salt with the fore-finger and thumb of his left hand.

"Ah!" said Sullivan, his pale face brightening. "I'm glad you have taken notice of me. Salt in large quantities, let me tell you, is the grand secret of long life and health. I use it with everything now—food and drink. When I wake up in the

night I swallow big spoonfuls of it. I know 'tis
a bit nasty until you get used to it. But there's
nothing good in the world that isn't nasty."

"You must have the stomach of a horse and
the brains of an ass!" exclaimed Carmody, with a
grimace.

"Try a little of it, Pat," said Sullivan coax-
ingly.

"Take it away man, take it away!" cried Carmody, drawing back his chair.

"Oh, you needn't be frightened," smiled Sullivan
—"but," in a serious and impressive tone, "you
may believe me this is the grandest medicine in
the world," pocketing the lump of salt. "And I
can tell you more, boys," he continued; "salt-water
baths—none of your common salt water, but thick,
heaps of salt, regular brine—them are the things
for health. I intend having a pickle bath every
morning ashore for the future."

"You'll be petrifying yourself one of those fine
days," snorted Broaders.

"Or turning yourself into a pillar of salt," added
Bendall, with a chuckle.

Captain Flynn had entered the room as Bendall

spoke, and, without saluting the assembled mariners, he exclaimed,—

"Fie, fie, Tom! How dare you give way to this wretched blasphemy? Don't you know well, Tom, that you're talking out of Holy Writ when you speak of pillars of salt."

"Oh dear, oh dear!" chuckled Bendall. "'Tis a pillar of the church you ought to be yourself. Sit down, Captain Flynn, and make yourself comfortable. What will you drink?"

The Bishop placed his umbrella behind the half-open door, drew off his heavy woollen gloves, advanced to the fireplace, and murmured in a reverential tone,—

"I think I'll try a little gin and water—very weak, Tom."

"Have a lump of Sullivan's salt in it, will you?" asked Bendall, making a mental note as to the position of the Bishop's umbrella. "A glass of gin, if you please, Miss Julia," nodding to the landlady, who entered the room after Flynn.

"Yes, try a little of it in your grog," cried Sullivan, taking the salt from his pocket and offering it to the bewildered Flynn. "I have discovered—"

"Oh, don't be for ever pestering us with your crazes!" exclaimed Carmody angrily. "Now, I tell you, if you say another word about salt in my presence, I'll knock you down. Mark me now."

"Gentlemen, gentlemen," murmured the Bishop, "I'm fairly surprised at you. 'Let dogs,' as some holy poet says, 'delight to bark and bite, but grown men should be different quite.'—Thank you, Miss Julia," to the landlady, who now handed him a glass. "So your good brother has gone from amongst us to-day."

"Yes, Captain Flynn. He ought to make a quick run this time. The wind is still blowing strong from the east."

"I wouldn't be surprised, though, if there was a shift before long," put in Bendall, who was anxious to find an excuse for getting nearer to Flynn's umbrella. "I wonder how is the glass," rising and approaching the barometer, of which he seemed to make an intent and prolonged study.

"By the way, Miss Julia," said the Bishop, "wasn't that young Mr Madden I saw leaving the house just as I was coming in?"

"Yes," stammered the landlady. "He was looking for the skipper of that Italian barque lying near the bridge. He's a nice young gentleman— I mean Mr Madden."

"Upstart," snorted Broaders.

"Puppy," snarled Carmody.

"Fie, fie! gentlemen," said the Bishop, waving his hand. "You should never speak badly of the absent when they're not present. Oh, Miss Julia, I knew there was something I had to say to you. I observed my mate at the counter outside. That man is a shocking ruffian when he drinks too much. Oblige me by giving him nothing stronger than ginger wine this evening; for he has a heavy family depending on him, a very heavy family, Miss Julia; and I want him to be at his work early in the morning. What a curse drink is!" he sighed, taking a mouthful of his gin.

"All right, Captain Flynn. I'll look after him, and see that he doesn't get intoxicated here at any rate."

"It's your turn to stand now, Captain Augy," snorted Broaders. "All our glasses are running dry."

"Well, gentlemen, name your drinks individually to Miss Julia."

"Same again!" chorused all the skippers, except Arkwright, who was fast asleep; and the landlady left the room.

"Charming creature!" smiled Cummins, who had been twirling his thumbs and staring with a vacant stare into the fire until the cry of "Same again," in which he had automatically joined, aroused him.

"Getting pretty well up in years now," snorted Broaders.

"Ah! if she would only try large quantities of salt!" sighed Sullivan.

"Oh, I wasn't thinking of Miss Julia," explained the now wide-awake Cummins. "I was thinking of John M'Cormick's wife."

"'Pon my song, Martin Cummins, you're a queer fish," laughed Bendall, who had by this time succeeded in concealing under his long pilot-cloth overcoat the Bishop's umbrella, and stood leaning against the corner of the mantelpiece. "What's coming over you at all?"

"Mind your own business, Bendall!" exclaimed Cummins angrily.

"Did you begin to load yet, Tom?" asked Flynn,

dreading high words, and therefore anxious to divert the current of the conversation.

"No, skipper. We're not out of the doctor's hands yet; and I fear we'll have to rip the decks out of her after all."

Here Miss Walsh entered the Nest with a tray, and handed the glasses round to the skippers.

"Mind what I told you about my mate, Miss Julia. I hope you're watching him, for he's a shocking blackguard when he gets too much drink aboard."

"I'm looking after him, Captain Flynn," smiled Miss Walsh, leaving the room.

"Now, look here, Bendall," cried Cummins, who had been gradually making up his mind to put a stop to Bendall's impertinence, "let me tell you once for all, sir, that I won't have you trying to poke your fun at me. Remember who you are, and who I am, sir. You're a fellow—I say it before all the gentlemen here," he went on rapidly and excitedly—"who hasn't got a certificate; and I have one, sir. If anybody doubts my word, here it is," fumbling in his breast-pocket and producing a dirty, greasy parchment. "I'm a captain, sir, a

captain—a title you have no right to, Tom Bendall, let me tell you."

The majority of coasting skippers of a past genera-
tion were uncertified master - mariners; and those
who possessed either a certificate of competency or
a certificate of service were mightily vain of the
possession, many of them fully believing they had
as much right, legally and morally, to the title
of captain as an officer wearing Her Majesty's
uniform.

Bendall laughed, and taking off his hat made a low
bow to Cummins. The action jerked the handle of
Flynn's umbrella through the breast of Captain
Tom's coat. He hastily tried to cover the handle,
but the Bishop caught a glimpse of his beloved
"crozier," and, jumping to his feet, he tore open
Bendall's coat, and pulled the umbrella forth from
its hiding-place. All the skippers burst forth into
noisy laughter, caused partly by Bendall's discomfi-
ture and partly by the exhibition of Flynn's wrath.
Even the slumbering Arkwright bobbed his head
up and down and smiled inanely in his sleep.

"It's a shame, Tom; a downright, dirty shame,"
fumed the Bishop. "A man might as well be

preaching sermons to milestones as trying to knock common sense and common decency into your empty brains."

"I couldn't help it, neighbour. Indeed I couldn't," murmured Bendall apologetically, but scarcely able to smother a laugh. "'Pon my song, I meant no harm. I wish to Heaven, Captain Augy, you'd burn the crozier, and take the temptation out of my road."

The Bishop sat down and turned his back towards Bendall, and tapping his teeth with ●his finger-nails, exclaimed,—

"'Tis the height of ignorance—the height of ignorance. There's neither sense nor meaning in your empty brains, Captain Bendall."

"Tom, you're a queer fellow," chuckled Cummins, determined now to apologise in a roundabout fashion for the insult he had a short time previously offered Bendall.

"Well, boys," said Bendall, "I am sorry for my bad behaviour. And I can tell you all that there isn't a man coming into this port, or into any other port, for the matter of that, I have a greater regard for than Augy Flynn."

"You're a queer fellow, Tom," again chuckled Cummins, scarcely knowing how to show he was sorry for his conduct, while sustaining at the same time the superiority of his position. "I hope you bear me no ill-will, Tom, on account of my remarks a short time ago. There's not a man in the room, let me tell you, barring myself and Augy Flynn, that's got a certificate any more than yourself; but for all that I hope I didn't hurt your feelings, Tom?"

"Not in the least," said Bendall. "When I put as many ships ashore as you have put, maybe I'll be looking to the Board of Trade myself for a ticket."

"I consider you have a great deal of impudence, Bendall, to attempt to address me in that fashion," snarled Cummins. "But," with a sneer, "what can you expect from a man who hasn't a certificate?"

"Miss Julia," cried Bendall to the landlady, who had entered the room in response to a summons from the bell, "we'll all have our glasses filled again—don't mind Captain Arkwright's as he isn't done snoring yet. And, Miss Julia, you might put a taste of ginger into Captain Cummins' grog. He looks as if he wanted something to warm him, poor fellow! Look how pale he is! I'm sure the man is love-sick."

"Tom, you're a queer fellow," laughed Cummins. "Isn't he, my dear?" to the landlady.

"Captain Cummins," said Miss Walsh, "I do wish you would keep your proper distance, and address me by my proper name;" and the land-lady flounced out of the room.

"Well, well," muttered Cummins, "the contrariness of females is something wonderful. That woman is becoming as high and mighty as Mrs M'Cormick herself. Ah!" his mouth broadening with a grin, "all that tossing of the head is put on just because there's a lot of you boys here. When I come in by myself there's a lump of differ-ence in Miss Julia's manners, I can tell you. Now it was only the other day—"

Here he suddenly stopped as Miss Walsh entered the room with the liquor. She scowled at Cummins, and retired to the shop without addressing a word to any of the skippers.

"Miss Julia is quite right," said Bendall. "I don't think a certified man ought to be insinuating that he's thinking of getting a third wife before

Number two is a twelvemonth under the sod.
How much, now, if it is a fair question, do the
undertakers allow you off the regulation charges,
Captain Cummins, or is the work done by con-
tract for you?"

"Tom, you're a queer fellow," laughed Cummins,
who was rather vain of having outlived two help-
mates.

"I wish you had more ballast in you, Tom,"
said the Bishop, turning round. He had now recovered from his fit of ill-humour. "You mean
well, I'm sure; but life is too serious a matter for
this constant frivolity. You can't expect to live
for ever in this vale of tears—"

"Try large quantities of salt," put in Sullivan,
eagerly.

"So help me!" cried Carmody, breaking off
abruptly a conversation with Broaders, "I'll not
stand your infernal nonsense any longer, skipper
Sullivan. No sooner are you done pestering us
with one craze than you start another. Last voyage you nearly drove me mad with some rubbish
about lucifer matches. Have done now: do you
mind me?"

"Oh! ho! ho!" yawned Arkwright, awaking from slumber and stretching out his arms. "Why, bless me!" he cried, rubbing his eyes, "I must have been ingratiating myself with a prolonged repose."

"Oh, don't mention it," drawled Bendall.

"Why, in Heaven's name, can't you talk plain?" asked Carmody.

"Talk plain," laughed Arkwright, a contemptuous, dignified laugh. "I flatter myself, sir, my discourse is homely, scholarly, and gentlemanly. When my late lamented parent on the male side was building—"

"Castles in the air. What a pity you didn't stick to carrying a hod yourself!"

"Sir," said Arkwright, with asperity, "your language is ignorant and unseemly. You seem constantly oscillating between ignorance and unseemliness, and verging on downright insolence."

"Why didn't they send you into Parliament? 'Tis a shocking loss to the country."

"I flatter myself I should not disgrace the first assemblage of European gentlemen," smiled Arkwright, twirling his thumbs.

"Well, don't be pestering us with your dictionary words, anyhow. I can tell you it isn't manners to be trying to choke yourself with jawbreakers every time you open your mouth."

"Oh, gentlemen, gentlemen," expostulated the Bishop, "let us change the subject; for it seems to me that some of you are slowly but surely drifting into abusive language—and it ill becomes you, Captain Carmody, to be constantly hurting the feelings of your neighbours. Fie, fie! Pat."

"I quite agree with you, Captain Augy," said Bendall. "Let us talk of something more pleasant than Sullivan's salt and Arkwright's book-learning. There's my friend Cummins there, thinking to himself as hard as he can. Now, I'll take my davy he's wondering which of his numerous lady friends will be the next Mrs Cummins. Am I right, skipper?"

"Tom, you're a queer fellow. There's no use at all in trying to be vexed with you. Put it there, Tom."

And Cummins and Bendall shook hands warmly.

"I wonder," snorted Broaders, "did big Mac get out of the harbour on the ebb?"

" Of course he did!" exclaimed Carmody. " What's to hinder him, with a tug boat ahead of him to drag him out?"

" What a charming example of femininity his good wife is!" said Arkwright. " Superior personage! What an expensive education she must have been inculcated with!"

" Ay! boarding-school education," snarled Carmody, as if some one had offered him a personal insult. " Boarding schools, indeed! where they teach girls to scratch the strings of a harp. and sew alphabets on canvas. 'Twould be fitter for them to show them how to darn a man's socks and sew buttons on his shirt, I can tell you."

" You're a vulgar, unintellectual specimen of humanity," said Arkwright contemptuously.

" Ah, don't be bothering us, man, with your cackling! I'm sick and tired, I am, of listening to your noise."

" If you're sick, skipper," began Sullivan, " try large—"

" I'll choke you with your own salt if you say another word!" cried Carmody, his eyes blazing with fire.

"Oh dear! oh dear!" laughed Bendall. "You're a nice agreeable lot of companions. You're after disgusting our friend the Bishop altogether."

"You never said a truer word, Tom. It's quite disgraceful to hear grown men squabbling in a Christian land. I'm ashamed of you, Pat. We all have our little failings; and I'd be the last man to fling the stone ; but your temper, Captain Carmody, is something fulsome."

"For half the complement of insulting observations you have addressed to me, sir," said Arkwright, gaining courage at the Bishop's speech, "you would, in some countries, find yourself incarcerated within the precincts of a miserable dungeon, where—"

"Oh dear! oh dear!" interrupted Bendall; "your remarks, skipper Arkwright, are heavy enough to sink a lifeboat. Take a sip out of your grog before you choke yourself right out."

For several minutes there was silence in the Nest. The silence was broken by the Bishop.

"Oh! ho! ho!" he yawned, taking out his watch and replacing it in his fob; "it's time to be going, gentlemen."

The mariners all stretched out their arms and yawned vigorously. Then each man stooped and drew down the legs of his trousers.

"I'm going your way, Jim," said Carmody to Sullivan.

Both men rose, and yawning again, stamped noisily on the floor.

"Give us a hornpipe before you go, Pat," said the Bishop.

"Ah, not to-night," smiled Carmody, stamping again. "I'm too stiff in the joints. Some other time."

"Well, we'll excuse you to-night, Pat, as it is so late," said the Bishop, rising; "but I'll stand no nonsense next time. Come along, Martin," tapping Cummins on the shoulder. "We have no home but our ships, so let us bear one another company down the quay."

All the skippers had now risen from their seats.

"Captain Bendall," said Arkwright, "our homes are located in the same direction, and yours, too, Captain Broaders."

"Don't forget your umbrella," cried Bendall, as

the Bishop and Cummins were about to leave the room.

"Thank you for the reminder, Tom ; I have it in my hand."

And the symposium at the Nest was broken up.

CHAPTER VII.

AFTER LONG YEARS.

MRS M'CORMICK was in an unusually excitable mood the morning after the departure of the *Water Nymph.* The previous evening she had been dull and depressed beyond measure, and had spent a restless, sleepless night. Her husband's words and manner had left a strong impression upon her. She felt her conduct towards M'Cormick during their seven years of married life had been unjust and cruel, and she was full of good resolutions for the future. She would endeavour to begin life anew—to forget the past and everything belonging to it. She hoped, she prayed they would go far away from Slough-ford—the change of scene would be certain to effect a change in herself.

But with the morning came the reaction.

After breakfast she sat at the window of the sitting-room, which overlooked the river, and struggle
as she might with herself, she could not shut out
memories of many years ago. With tears coursing
slowly down her cheeks she remained for a long
time—she knew not how long—gazing at the ships
and barges sailing up with the tide. Then, as she
rose from her chair, her eyes caught the outline of
the old wooden bridge, and with a smothered sob
she turned away her head and began to pace up
and down the room, her hands clasped tightly in
front of her.

"My God, my God!" she cried, "I thought I had
lived it down. I wonder if I shall ever see him
again,—ever know if he has forgiven me. What
have I done that all my life should be spoiled, all
the sunshine and happiness taken out of it?"

She stopped abruptly as she passed the window,
and stood staring in the direction of the bridge.

"Oh! I am a fool—I am worse. It is sinful
as well as silly to give way to such thoughts.
She sank into a seat, a sad smile curving her
mouth. "I wonder what would poor John say if

he were only to see me playing tragedy just now, and know what my thoughts were. I must not allow myself to think of the past ever again. I must, I will, shut my eyes to it. I have been too much alone latterly. I suppose that is why I am so low-spirited. I wonder Helen has not come over to see me. I must write to her."

She got up and went through the half - open folding-doors into the adjoining room. This room overlooked the garden, and in it Mrs M'Cormick usually spent the better part of the day. But now the river had a fascination for her, and as if she were performing some guilty deed she brought a small writing-desk stealthily from the inner room and placed it on a table near the window.

As she was about to sit down, the sound of footsteps crunching the gravel outside reached her ears. Looking through the curtains, she stood for a moment breathless, her eyes almost bursting from their sockets, and her face pale as a winding-sheet. Then the blood rushed quickly to her cheeks, and with a low cry—half sob, half moan— she started back, pressing her palms to her throbbing temples.

Ere she had time to regain self-possession, her visitor was announced, and stood in the room close to her.

She turned round, her cheeks still scarlet, her heart throbbing violently, and stretched out her hand in silence.

Her visitor grasped the extended hand, and said in a grave, quiet tone,—

"You are astonished to see me again. I do not wonder. Believe me, I never meant to meet you, but fate—I suppose I must call it fate—sent me here."

"Sit down, won't you?" said Mrs M'Cormick, motioning him to a chair near the fireplace: her visitor's coldness put her almost at her ease. "You won't mind my finishing this note, I hope. I am in a hurry to send it to the post."

Without waiting for any reply, she took up her pen and began to write. If her visitor had watched her closely, he could see that her fingers trembled so violently that she could scarcely hold the pen.

After a few minutes, during which time the pulsing of her heart had gradually ceased to be a serious trouble to her, she folded the note and placed it in an envelope. Then she asked her visitor to ring the bell. A ruddy-cheeked, healthy-looking young woman entered the room. Mrs M'Cormick closed the desk, and handed the note to a young woman, her maid. She was quite at ease now ; quite at ease.

" He doesn't care in the least for me. He has been wiser than I. He has lived it down. Thank God ! "

" Well, Mr Dalton," she began,—

" Don't, please," he interrupted, with a trace of bitterness. " It almost makes me laugh to hear you call me Mr Dalton ; and "—his voice growing more gentle—" it sounds too brutally cold after all these years. You never called me so in all your life before."

" But everything has altered very much since I saw you last."

" Yes," he said, sadly and slowly. " I need scarcely be reminded of that."

" I wonder you recognised me. People tell me I have altered considerably during the past five or six years. Sometimes when I look in the glass I fancy I am quite forty—and I'm not quite forty yet," she added, with a feeble attempt at a smile.

" No. You will be only twenty-seven next May—
the fifth of May, is it not ? "

" What a memory you have ! "

" Yes," quite softly. " A long memory for some
things, Susie."

" Don't; for God's sake don't call me that !" she
gasped, involuntarily pressing her fingers to her
eyes. " No one has ever called me Susie since a
certain night long ago—when—when—O God ! help
me, I cannot bear it all."

Here Mrs M'Cormick found that she could no
longer check her sobs, and rising hastily she went
to the window, and with tear-blinded eyes pressed
her cheeks to the cool window panes. After a few
moments she came back to her chair.

Dalton had in the meantime sat with folded arms,
staring moodily into the fire which flickered in the
small fire-grate.

" I am quite upset to-day," she said, breaking the
silence; " I have a bad headache, and my nerves are
all unstrung. I don't know what ails me. You
must not mind me. I shall be all right presently.
Tell me all about yourself. What have you been
doing ? What brings you to Sloughford ? "

"To tell you all about myself for the past seven or eight years—it will be eight years next August since I saw you last—would be tiresome and uninteresting, I fear, Mrs M'Cormick."

"You may call me by my Christian name if you like," she interrupted. "It will sound less strange in my ears —but," with a little gasp, "you must never do so again after to-day. I think I can promise you I won't feel uninterested in your story."

"Thank you. I haven't very much to tell, indeed ; but if you are sure I sha'n't bore you, I'll give you a very brief account of myself since I saw you last. May I go on ? "

"Yes. I suppose you are married ? "

She would have given worlds to recall the words as she looked at his face ; but she could not have restrained herself. She was burning with curiosity to know if he had entirely forgotten her,—if he had formed new ties more binding than the old ones.

"Married !" he said bitterly. "Didn't I tell you I had a long memory ? Why should I marry ? You are all alike. You love your ease ; you would do anything rather than endure a little worry—a little trouble. None of you know what love really means·

Love—what do you know of love, may I ask ? Oh !
I am sick of the word. I hate you all ; I despise you
all. You broke my heart, woman !"

He turned and looked at her fiercely. He had
determined to be cool and collected all through the
interview ; but now he found he had lost control
over himself. He was unable to keep back the tears
which welled into his eyes.

"Oh, Susie, Susie !" he cried piteously. "Why
could you not have waited for me ? I would have
worked for you, slaved for you, waited for you half
a lifetime. "What am I saying ?" he moaned, rising
from his chair and pacing up and down the room,
as Mrs M'Cormick had paced it a short time before.
"I am mad ; I thought I had forgotten you—or hated
you."

Fortunately for Mrs M'Cormick, she was struck by
the fact that his actions now resembled hers before
she had taken her writing-desk from the inner
room ; and this saved her from breaking down
utterly. She set herself thinking how curious it
was that in such a short space of time a man who
she thought had ceased to remember her existence,
and who, for aught she knew to the contrary, was

at the other end of the world, or dead, should almost imitate her words—yes, even her very actions. Then she fancied, or rather tried to fancy, he was burlesquing her movements. It was so funny. Yes, that was exactly the way she had stumbled against a chair. He stopped and looked out of the window. She had done the same. Could anything be more amusing?—and she burst into a hysterical fit of laughter.

He turned round, and laughed too—a strange hollow laugh, that sounded like mockery in her ears. Then he found she was crying bitterly.

"Susie, Susie," he said, approaching her, going down on one knee, and clasping her hand, "what is it? What have I said? I scarcely know, myself. Do forget my roughness—my pettishness. I could not help it. Do forgive me!"

She took her hand away, and motioned him to sit down. In silence he resumed his seat, and after a pause Mrs M'Cormick spoke,—

"We have both been very foolish just now, I fear. Please forget it all for ever. Promise me you will."

"Then you are not vexed with me?"

"No; but promise me you will forget all that has just happened. "I don't know what ails me this morning. I feel quite upset. Don't think I am always such a stupid person. You were going to tell me about yourself, when something interrupted you."

"You know a little of my story already. After I made up my mind to try what luck the sea would bring me, I went a long voyage, and on my return to Liverpool I got your last letter. I did not storm or rage at the awful news it told me, but I think it very nearly drove me mad. However, I'm not going to dwell upon that portion of the past. I determined to stick to the sea."

"How strange you should have gone to the sea! I hate the sea."

"I don't. I love it. After some six years of knocking about, I passed for master in the foreign trade. I had little difficulty in getting a ship out of Liverpool, owing to my father's connection there long ago. I entered Sloughford harbour yesterday in a barque of two thousand tons. You should just see my ship. All Sloughford was out this morning to look at her. They say she is the largest ship that ever came up to the quays."

"You seem quite enthusiastic about your profession."

"I am enthusiastic about it. I love my ship. She
is a beauty. She is my sweetheart and wife, and
there is no danger she will throw me over, so long
as I remain faithful to her."

"You are unkind, Dick. I did not throw you
over—if that is what you mean."

She bit her lip as she said this. The words had
been uttered without premeditation.

"Oh no! Of course you didn't. You simply did
what pleased you best. I do not blame you, I assure
you. No doubt you had almost forgotten the fact
of my existence."

He was again excited, and had apparently forgotten
his resolution and his promises.

"You should not talk to me like that, nor should I
have said to you half the things I have said. You
must not attempt to refer to the past again."

She spoke hurriedly and sharply, her cheeks
glowing, and her eyes dilated and wild looking.

"Forgive me! I forgot myself. I know I have
no right to come here and whine. I am ashamed of
myself. I fancied I had no place in your memory.

Why should I have any; or why should you be annoyed when I say so?"

She was softened by his quiet tone, in which she could trace a cry of despair.

"You are cruel," she murmured. "You know it broke my heart, too. Every word of my last letter to you was true, bitterly true—but is it right we should speak to one another thus? Let us bury the past for ever."

"I cannot truthfully promise you that. Believe me, though, I did not mean to break down as I have done — I am disgusted with my weakness, my unmanliness. But memories crowded in upon me so thick—"

"You must banish these memories. You must promise me you will never in any way allude to what has passed between us now or long ago. If you do not promise, I swear I shall never open my lips to you again. Do you realise my position and yours?"

"I promise. But you need not think I intend to persecute you with reproaches. Perhaps we may never meet again after to-day."

After a pause.

" How did you find me out ? Did Mr Butler
give you my address ? "

" No—but how stupid of me ! I have almost lost
sight of the object of my visit here. When my
ship was coming into the harbour yesterday, we
met a barque sailing out—the *Water Nymph*—
your husband's ship."

" Yes, my husband's ship. Surely my husband
did not send you here ? "

" Strangely enough, he did—with a message."

" You astonish me. I should have thought •you
would be about the last person in the world he
would have selected to convey a message to me."

" Why ? " with a smile.

She was vexed for having spoken, and for the
evident assumption on Dalton's part that her husband still had cause to remember that Dalton and
she had once been sweethearts.

" You are wrong," she said scornfully. " You need
not think he has ever had cause to remember—anything. But I know he always disliked you, because
you were what he calls a fine gentleman."

Dalton was nettled by the answer, and bit his lip
at the words " fine gentleman."

"I am a fine gentleman no longer," he said. "I am only a master-mariner—just a trifle better than a common sailor."

"You don't look a bit like one, at anyrate," she smiled. "No one alive would take you for a sailor."

"I don't know whether you intend to be' complimentary or the reverse—"

"Pray do not let us squabble," she cried impatiently. "I was not thinking of compliments or insults. Please tell me about the message from my husband."

"He sent you this," taking a letter from the breast-pocket of his coat, and handing the letter to Mrs M'Cormick. "He did not know that I would be the bearer of the note," he explained. "He left it with the master of the pilot-cutter, and told him to give it to the captain of the first ship entering the harbour, and to ask that captain to deliver the letter with his own hands. So now you know why it is that I have come here this morning. Otherwise I should never have crossed your threshold."

"I expect you were surprised when you read the address on the envelope. How strange!" dreamily.

" ' Surprised ' is scarcely a strong enough word. But," rising, " I have paid you an unconscionably long visit. My ship will be a month here discharging. Shall I see you before I sail ? " forgetful once more of his resolutions never to look again at the woman who had jilted him.

" I don't know. You must never see me alone again. But you know Helen Cadogan, do you not ? "

" Butler's niece ? Yes, I think I remember her. She was at school somewhere when I left Sloughford. Butler will introduce me to her if she has forgotten me. He is doing the business of my ship here, of course."

" We visit one another occasionally. If she and her uncle accompany you, I don't think I would have any objection to seeing you."

" You are very kind." There was a touch of sarcasm in his voice. Her coldness chilled him. " Good-bye," he said, holding out his hand.

And then as he looked at her and reflected it was the last time they might meet alone again, and that their paths in this world lay wider apart than ever, a strange longing to kiss her lips, to hold her in his arms once more, even were it only for an instant, seized him. Instinctively Mrs M'Cormick divined his thoughts. Rising, she rang a small handbell which lay on the table, and then opening the door of the sitting-room smiled,—

"Don't mind my turning you out so abruptly. 1 had no notion it was so late; and I have a visit to pay in the neighbourhood this afternoon."

He seized her hand and raising it to his lips, cried,—

"Susie—for the last time, Susie—good-bye!"

"Good-bye," she murmured, pressing his hand. "Good-bye."

When the door closed after him she burst into a passionate fit of weeping.

"I must never see him again. Never, never. May God pity me and forgive me—for I love him still! I love him, God help me!"

Part the Second.

A MESSAGE FROM THE DEEP.

CHAPTER I.

INTRODUCES ONE OF THE SMARTEST CRAFTS AFLOAT, AND ONE OF THE SMARTEST OF SKIPPERS.

ABOUT three weeks after the *Water Nymph* sailed from Sloughford, a strange brigantine was observed making for the entrance of that harbour, and the pilot-cutter swiftly bore down upon her and put a man in charge.

"Twelve days from St John's, Newfoundland, captain! Why, a steamboat might with reason be proud of a passage like that. 'Tis a clipper she is, an' no mistake!"

"Right, sonny! Guess you'll find there ain't

many smarter crafts afloat than the *Greenback*, of St John, New Brunswick, nor many smarter men than Angus R. Nixon—that's me, pilot."

The first speaker was the sea pilot who had just been hoisted on board the *Greenback*, and the second speaker was the master of that rakish-looking craft.

Angus R. Nixon might indeed be justly proud of his vessel, and justly elated at having made such a rapid passage across the Atlantic, for it would not be easy to find a neater-looking trading brigantine; and a twelve days' sail from St John's, Newfoundland, to the south coast of Ireland was, as Captain Nixon would term it, "doing it pretty tidy," even with the assistance of strong westerly winds and a buoyant cargo—oil in casks and dried cod-fish.

Nixon was five feet ten inches in height, and thirty-four years of age. He had high cheek bones, lantern jaws, a straight nose of a purple hue, a wide mouth, a long upper-lip, restless grey eyes, and a narrow forehead. His raven black hair was allowed to wander below his coat collar, and was carefully oiled. He was clean shaven, and his chin rivalled his nose in the depth of its purple tint.

Nixon had been taught the business of seamanship in the worst school afloat. From the age of twelve until, in the natural course of things, he left the forecastle to become one of the "after guard," he had been accustomed to the roughest usage, the most unseaworthy vessels, and the companionship of the most degraded and reckless class of seamen. He had been badly fed, badly paid, and worked like a galley slave; so it was not a matter for wonder that noble sentiments, noble aspirations, and noble deeds had no place in the mechanism of Angus R. Nixon. Still he seemed to thrive. "Only a copper-fastened constitution, bolted through and through, could have comed right straight along as I have comed," he would often remark.

As a matter of course, he made a most tyrannical mate, and was cordially detested by the fo'c'stle hands. It must not be supposed he was more tyrannical than hundreds of other mates— very likely he was not nearly so overbearing as many—but certainly he was held in greater detestation by sailors than the bulliest of "bully mates." The principal cause of the hatred arose from the fact that Angus was a cheat and a coward. Few sailors would have thought very badly of him for being a bit of a cheat, perhaps; fewer still would have blamed him for being a tyrant; but no sailor has any affection or respect for a combination of cheat and coward.

It seemed as if Nixon lived chiefly for the pleasure of cheating. His essays in this line too, were, it must be confessed, of the meanest kind. He was too cowardly to be a cheat of dangerous proportions. It would afford him greater delight to earn a penny dishonestly than to earn a pound honestly; and he would at any time prefer to throw away a pound than to allow any one to diddle him out of a penny.

He got into trouble afloat and ashore times without number; but as his attempts at obtaining money or advantages dishonestly were always conducted on so diminutive a scale, and he was such a cringing coward whenever he was found out, few had ever thought to "make an example" of him.

About eight months before the arrival of the *Green-*

back in Sloughford harbour, Nixon was serving as first mate on board a North American timber trader, and this ship was fortunate enough in mid-Atlantic to fall in with a derelict barque laden with cotton. It was fine weather, and the crew of the timber trader succeeded in bringing their prize, which had evidently been abandoned too early, safe into port. Nixon's portion of the salvage was sufficient to supply him with the purchase-money of a brigantine, called the *Cordelia*, carrying about two hundred and twenty tons, and also enabled him to spend a large sum of money on re-decking, refastening, and generally overhauling the brigantine.

He did not like the name of his purchase; he could not imagine what Cordelia meant; and he did not care to run the risk of being laughed at for his ignorance. He consulted several learned nautical men, and after having made them too jolly to be captious, he asked them what a cordelia was.

Most of them shook their heads. One of them thought it was a foreign name for a small rope; another fancied it was the name of a chain of mountains; another was almost certain it was an

Italian word for ginger wine. The most learned of
the learned mariners, a grave and reverend signior
of sixty, asked for time to hunt up the word.

"Without committing myself, I reckon it's a word
for a sort of flower; but I have some dictionaries
and things in my state-room, Nixon," said he, "and
you just hold on till to-morrow, and I'll tell you
what it means right straight away."

The old man met Nixon the next day with a
beaming countenance.

"I've discovered the secret, my boy. I've wormed
it out," he cried. "There ain't nothing like books
arter all when a man's in a quandary. And what
do you think, my boy: they've gone and spelt the
dashed name wrong. Blest if they ain't! Sich
ignorance, when a man has only to look a thing
up! C-o-r-d-e-l-i-e-r—that's how to spell it. It's a
nickname for a lot of old monks. That's what it is."

"Old monks!" ejaculated Nixon scornfully. "I'll
have none of their sort on the stern of my ship,
you bet. Now, skipper, tell me what in your
opinion's the most beautiful thing in nater?"

"Greenbacks, sonny. Greenbacks," replied the
maritime bookworm, who hailed from Boston city.

"P'raps you're right," drawled Nixon. "P'raps you ain't. For my part, I prefers a plain, straight up and down British sovereign; but as you've said 'Greenbacks,' and as you've warned me off those cussed monks, as ain't fish, fowl, or good red herring, why I'll get my craft rechristened *The Greenback*, for I calculate she'll be about the next most beautiful thing in nater when I takes her out of dry dock."

Although he spoke jauntily, and with apparent cheerfulness, about the purchase of the brigantine, still a canker-worm was gnawing at Nixon's heart. It was ever present to his mind that he had obtained the salvage money through no special skill of his own,—that his meeting with the derelict ship was merely a piece of good luck which might have fallen to the least wide-awake of mariners. This wounded his sense of vanity; for, considering that, according to his own estimate, he was the most cunning tar who ever boxed a compass, it was rather rough upon him that he had never been able to save money by his cunning. And the weakest point in Nixon's mental armour was his vanity. He was vain of everything connected with himself — vain of his conversational powers, vain of his adroitness, vain even of his personal appearance, which was scarcely prepossessing. Any one who thought it worth while to pander to Nixon's vanity found little difficulty in smiting him hip and thigh.

After the *Greenback* had taken on board, at St John's, the cargo of fish and oil, Captain Nixon determined he would go in for cheating on a higher scale than heretofore.

" I'll fly for higher game, I will," he chuckled. " I'll astonish the half-dead-and-alive sogers I come across, I will. When I get my headpiece in proper working order, you may bet your life Captain Kidd will be a trifle to leeward in some respects of Angus R. Nixon. Yes, siree."

The *Greenback's* passage across the Atlantic had been so rapid that the skipper found he had scarcely sufficient time for planning any special cheating campaign against the first shore folk he would meet—the Sloughfordians. He was almost sorry when he saw the Sloughford pilot-boat bearing down upon him.

" Dang it ! " he muttered ; " say as they may,

''tis a good wind blows nobody ill.' A touch of a nor'-easter would have given me a darned sight more time to think out how I am to get clear of this port with flying colours. 'Tis a bit strange, it is, that a smart man like me thinks so tarnation slow; but when I think a thing out, you bet there ain't many as can act as quick. I'd just like, I would, to fleece every mother's son of 'em in this 'ere port—and I'll do it, too, when my brain gets into proper working order, after the anchor's down."

When the pilot got on board he stood hard by the wheel, and to Captain Dixon's delight, was evidently lost in amazement at the brightness of everything around him, and at the beauty of the curve in the *Greenback's* decks, for even a sea pilot can admire the line of beauty. After Angus had, with a constrained effort of modesty, declared that there not many smarter men afloat than he, the pair were silent for some minutes.

"What sort of a port is yourn?" asked the skipper, breaking the silence, "for I reckon I'm a stranger here, and"—with a guffaw—"you mustn't go risking your salvations trying to take me in."

"Well then, sir, I may tell you, and tell no lie, that it is the finest and honestest port that a vessel ever dropped her anchor in. Fine-aisy goin' people everywhere, and heaps of water. You could lay afloat, in a manner of speaking, chock alongside the quays; but no doubt, captain, you'll be discharging at a wharf, and there, at any rate, you'll have twenty feet under you at low water."

"I'm glad to hear that, pilot; for I wouldn't care to let my craft touch the ground for a consideration. She's that sharp, she is, she'd heel right over if she tried to lay aground. That's so, pilot."

"Ah, 'tis a beauty she is, captain. I fancies this minute 'tis aboard a yacht I am; and 'tisn't every day you come across a fine, handsome gentleman like yourself even in the grandest of yachts. I suppose now she's a purty strong draught of water, your honour?"

"You bet. She's a good thirteen feet aft this minute."

"Well, that's a comfort anyhow, skipper; for you see we're paid accordin' to the draught of water. and when you runs over twelve feet they puts you on a higher scale. Thirteen feet! I'd have gone away contented with ten feet on my ticket, I would; but you see how aisy it is to be mistaken! There isn't a man born would think she'd go over ten feet, to look at her in the trim she is."

Captain Nixon could scarely contain his rage. He had been quite under the impression that pilotage fees in Sloughford harbour were chargeable on the tonnage of the ship, and he had unwittingly stated his real draught of water. In ports where pilotage fees are chargeable on the draught, it was quite a common practice to give a false return, and both harbour authorities and pilots were either too indolent or too unsuspicious to "hook" a strange vessel. A clever pilot generally contrived to ascertain the real draught in a roundabout, inoffensive way.

"Guess you chaps here are too smooth-faced for me, pilot," said Nixon, after a long pause. "If your townies are all as honest as you, a fellow will have to keep his weather eye open very wide."

"Honest, captain! Why, there is as unsuspecting and as decent a crowd along the quays of the town as ever drew the breath of life. An infant might play with 'em!"

Nixon paused again and took a careful survey of the pilot, who looked as childlike and bland as the "Heathen Chinee." The pilot, thinking that the skipper was evidently not quite satisfied about the honesty and guilelessness of the Sloughfordians, burst out with,—

"You seems to doubt me, captain. I declare to you, if you were to lie asleep on the quays with your mouth open, there isn't a soul in the place would steal a tooth out of your head—and 'that's what you can't say of every port."

Captain Nixon seemed more puzzled than ever. "Those Sloughfordians," he thought, "are either about as smart as they make 'em, or else they're the most con-founded set of idiots that ever breathed; but trust me to take their bearings. I rather reckon I'll get a trifle to wind'ard of them before they see the last of the *Greenback.*"

"Waal, pilot, I'll just go below and have a bit of a wash-up before the tug boat gets a grip of our rope."

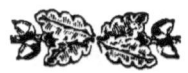

CHAPTER II.

LOST, OR NOT LOST?

WHEN the brigantine was approaching the town, a small boat came alongside, and Madden and Ryan clambered up the side of the *Greenback*.

"Waal," asked Captain Nixon, who was now, with brightly scrubbed face, standing on the poop, "what's your business, gents? I'm the boss of this show."

"Good morning, captain," said Madden. "We represent Butler, Mr James Butler, ship-agent; and," tendering a card, "we have come to ask you for the ship's business."

"Oh!" drawled Nixon. "That's your game, is it? Waal, gents, I ain't going to give you my business, so you can hook it over the side as quick as you like. I was recommended at St John's to another broker—Thornhill by name."

"Thornhill?" exclaimed Madden, frowning. "Thornhill? Are you quite sure that's the name? Thornhill!"

"Quite sure, sonny. I have got it wrote down in black and white, I have."

"Thornhill," repeated Madden. Turning to his fellow-clerk, who stood silently at his side, "Ryan, have ever heard of a Mr Thornhill, a shipbroker in Sloughford? I need scarcely ask you, but I never like to be too positive about things."

"Thornhill?" said Ryan, in a weak, faltering tone; "no, I don't think I ever heard the name."

"Oh, you must be making some mistake, captain," addressing himself again to Nixon. "If there were such a man, it would be impossible that neither of us should not have heard of him."

"Don't you fret, sonny. I wasn't born yesterday, nor the day before. I know my way about, I do. Thornhill is the name. I have got it wrote down, and Angus R. Nixon—that's me, stranger—ain't the sort of man to make a mistake over a name."

"Well, I am puzzled, I confess," said Madden, biting his thumb, and still frowning. "Thornhill, a shipbroker, in Sloughford!" Then, his countenance beaming with a smile, "By gad! you are right, captain. Of course I know the man you mean. Well, well, how stupid of me to forget! You must know, him, Ryan. Don't you remember that poor, broken-down old fellow, that has a sort of dungeon in an attic, which he calls an office? Ah! you must know him. Up a little side street off the quay he lives—you have to mount a ladder to get up to his attic. Think, man!"

"Now that you bring his place to my recollection, of course I remember the man."

"Of course. Oh! good morning, Captain Nixon," with a loud, mocking laugh; "I'd be very sorry to take anything out of that poor buffer's way. Poor old Thornhill! I ought to have remembered him at once—many a little job we gave him. But you put him out of my thoughts when you spoke of him as the ship agent who was about to transact the business of a vessel like yours. Oh, give him your business by all means, captain! You'll be as manna in the desert to the poor old fellow."

Nixon looked puzzled; Madden's apparent sincerity was fast telling upon him.

"Tell Thornhill we were aboard," went on Madden volubly, "but would not dream of interfering with him. Madden is my name, captain—Arthur Madden. I think we had better be on the move, Ryan. Well, good day, captain. I hope you're not scant of breath —you'll have plenty of exercise trying to mount to that attic of your agent's; it will be quite as good as a little ramble in the country. I think the ladder wants a rung or two near the top, but I'm not quite sure about that. However, you had better be careful, for it would be a serious matter for a heavy man like you to miss your footing—a broken neck is rather a large order. And," lowering his voice and adopting a confidential and condescending tone, "he'll want to make you stand him drinks till morning, but you must not listen to his palaver. Of course he can't advance you any money, but don't let that trouble you. If you should want a few pounds when you get your ship moored, don't be shy of coming to our office for it. My governor, James Butler—you will remember the name, I hope—wouldn't like to see a strange skipper in a fix. Poor old Thornhill! Come along, Ryan. We are taking up too much of Captain Nixon's valuable time."

"Stop!" cried Angus, completely befooled: "I don't want to put the business of my craft into the hands of any old, half-starved broker, with an office in an attic. I must see into this when I get ashore."

"Charity, Captain Nixon, charity," interrupted Madden. "You can take my word for it, you will be performing a noble act of self-sacrifice."

"Self-sacrifice be hanged! Business is business with Angus R. Nixon—that's me, gents. You just hang on here, and I think I'll make up my mind to fetch you my papers. You appear a pretty tidy sort of man, you do, Mr Madden."

"Really, captain," smiling, "you are too complimentary. I am sincerely obliged for your promise, but my governor would not think of injuring a poor old man like Thornhill. How stupid of us, Ryan, to forget the name when Captain Nixon mentioned it! No doubt he'll pull you through somehow at the Custom House, if he can manage to pick up any sort of a decent coat; but I must say it was not very nice of your friends at St John's to give you the old chap's name."

"My friends be hanged!" cried Nixon. "I'll take

precious good care I don't put any of my limbs out of joint by climbing up a rickety ladder."

"Well, if you are quite determined not to go to Thornhill, you can't do better than put your ship in our charge, captain. I would be the last in the world to interfere with your arrangements; but it would pain me to see a beautiful little craft like yours get into bad hands."

"Come below, gents," said Nixon, leading the way down the companion staircase.

Madden and Ryan followed the master of the *Greenback*, and the trio soon were seated around the cabin table.

"Anything strange or wonderful on the passage over?" inquired Madden, placing the ship's papers in the breast-pocket of his coat.

"Waal, not much," drawled Nixon, with a self-satisfied air. "We was in too big a hurry, we was, to trouble about anything—except it might be dodging the ice for a couple of days.—Ah, by-the-bye," he cried, standing up, "we fell in with some wreckage. I rather expect the crew of the ship it once belonged to are hobnobbing it now with old Davy Jones. Got foul of an iceberg, I reckon; and I ain't generally far astray in my reckonings. Come on deck, gents, and have a look at my bit of flotsam and jetsam."

Madden was now anxious to get away from the ship as quickly as possible, fearing Thornhill or one of his clerks might board her at any moment and create a little scene. However, he could not refuse to have a look at the wreckage picked up by the brigantine. So Nixon and the visitors went on deck.

Ryan remained near the companion in order to speak to the pilot, and Madden and the skipper walked to the main hatch.

On the deck, forward of the hatch, lay a large, ungainly slab of timber, apparently a portion of a ship's stern. Madden, who was a trifle near-sighted, stooped, and knelt on one knee in order to examine some letters which were painted on the timber.

Instantly he rose to his feet, alarm plainly depicted in his good-humoured face.

The master of the *Greenback* gazed in amazement at him.

Ryan, who had been walking slowly towards the main hatch, ran quickly forward when he saw his fellow-clerk jump to his feet.

"What's the matter?" asked Nixon and Ryan almost in the same breath.

"It is M'Cormick's ship!" exclaimed Madden. "Look, Ryan," pointing to the wreckage on the deck. "*WATER N*, and underneath, SLO. That's *Water Nymph*, of Sloughford. It must be."

Ryan stood staring stupidly at the letters painted on the rough, splintered slab of timber.

Turning to Nixon, who could not understand the cause of the sudden excitement, Madden, still pointing to the deck, explained,—

"There can be little doubt that you have picked up a portion of the stern of a barque hailing from this port. Do you really think she is lost?"

"Think!" said Nixon. "There ain't no thinking necessary. She's down among the dead men as sure as my name is Angus, and that's pretty sure, stranger. I picked up a lot of broken timber that was knocking about when we was a few days out from St John's; but I reckoned it wasn't no manner of use in holding on to anything as hadn't a clue to the vessel's name. I got rid of all the lumber except this bit. The ship that owned it once, you mark me, was broken into matches by the ice—the coon that sailed her kept too northerly a course, and perhaps a bad look-out. That's what he did. You look a trifle skeered, you do, young man."

"Yes; it gave me a bit of shock. Come along, Ryan. Good day, Captain Nixon," grasping the mariner's hand. "Our runner will meet you when you get ashore, and show you our office. We must be off now."

Madden turned to Ryan as he got into the boat, and said,—

"That's a strange piece of news, isn't it ? Now, don't you get telling every one about it. Try and keep your tongue quiet until to-morrow. Here, take the oars! I'll steer. Run her alongside the first landing-place we meet. I must see old Cheevers before he goes to press with to-morrow's 'Gazette.' Pull man! The New Brunswicker will be so busy mooring his ship, that it's a thousand to one he'll forget all about his bit of wreckage until he awakes in the morning. Old Cheevers ought to make a little sensation in his dead-and-alive old paper—bereaved and beautiful widow—afflicted sister—gallant but ill-fated mariner. Poor old Jack M'Cormick!"

" What a fellow you are, Madden!"

"Pull, man! We'll never get ashore at this rate. I'd like to see old Thornhill when he finds how beautifully we got to windward of him over the *Greenback*. He was speaking about her to me yesterday. You were very near selling me with your stupid replies. 'Oh, yes' — 'of course' — ' quite so.' Why can't you have more go in you? Why can't you pluck up courage for once in your life?"

"Thornhill will be punching your head one of these fine days, if you don't look out."

"Will he? Two could play at that game. Look at that for muscle!" laying his fingers on his arm. " Pull harder, can't you? Now then, a good, sweeping stroke. That's it. Bravo! Why, you'll be developing muscle yourself one of these fine days if you don't look out."

Ryan smiled feebly. His exertions with the oars were telling upon him rapidly. His cheeks were a bright red, and the sweat poured down his face. Laying down the oars, he panted,—

"You must give me a breathing space. I'm quite done up."

Madden did not offer to take the oars. He lolled on the stern, toying with the tiller of the boat.

"I'm just thinking," said Ryan, wiping his brow with his handkerchief, "that the governor will kick up a deuce of a row if he hears of the way you go on down the river. That New Brunswick skipper will be so vexed that he'll tell Thornhill all you said about him."

"Not he," smiled Madden. "You just leave Blue Nose to me. I'll make it right with him this evening before he pays a visit to the shore. I know the sort of man I have to deal with. I certainly shouldn't like the governor to be upset by any complaints from Thornhill. The governor is too absurdly particular. Conscience makes a regular coward of him. If it hadn't been for my bounce, we'd never have got the *Greenback's* papers."

"Talking of conscience," said Ryan shyly; "might I ask if you have a spark of it left?"

"Why, what on earth do you mean?"

"You know what I mean. Maggie is regularly breaking her heart." Lifting his head and looking defiantly at Madden: "You have no right to make a fool of her. I tell you I won't stand it."

He gripped the oars and began to pull slowly to the shore.

For a moment Madden felt, and looked, uneasy.

"Don't be interfering in what doesn't concern you," he cried, recovering himself. "What business have you to meddle with my affairs?"

"What business have I?" laughed the other scornfully. "I'll tell you what business I have. You have led her to believe you were going to marry her, and for some time you have been gradually trying to back out of your promises—I know the reason why. You need not think you'll frighten me now by glaring at me in that way. I'm too much in earnest. I tell you if you break my sister's heart, I'll be her avenger."

"You!"

"Yes. I."

"You are mad, Ryan. You don't know what you're saying, man. Look out! Quick. You'll run right into the landing-place. Back water— quick!"

CHAPTER III.

CONTAINS AN EXTRACT FROM THE " SLOUGHFORD
GAZETTE," AND RECORDS SOME CONVERSATION.

IN Princes Street were situated the offices
of the rival newspapers, the " Sloughford
Weekly Gazette" and the " Sloughford
Weekly Chronicle"—not that their rivalry was of
the ordinary kind, both journals being almost non-
political.

The " Gazette " lived by the shipping interest; the
" Chronicle " appealed chiefly to the shopkeepers and
to the farmers who dwelt in the neighbourhood of
Sloughford. The " Gazette " prided itself on its
intimate knowledge of shipping affairs. The
" Chronicle " occasionally attempted to be scholarly,
and when in this mood it endeavoured to secure
an aristocratic audience; but as the only aristocratic,

or would-be aristocratic, families of which the
town, or its neighbourhood, could boast were, or had
been, connected in some way with the sea, the
"Chronicle" in appealing to them was nothing if not
delicately flavoured with salt, and usually came to
grief over some intricate nautical point. The
"Gazette," on the other hand, occasionally attempted to discuss agricultural affairs, and when it
did so it fared no better than the "Chronicle" discussing matters maritime. It was on such occasions
that editorial venom was exhibited in its most
dangerous aspect; and sometimes the jeers and the
sneers of the rival editors resulted in quarrels which
threatened to assume alarming proportions.

The editor of the "Gazette," who was the proprietor of his paper, avowed an infinite contempt
for the editor of the "Chronicle," who was also
proprietor of *his* paper; and the latter gentleman
avowed an infinite contempt for the former. They
never met socially, and when business brought
them together, the only difficulty was to discover
which of the Sloughford men of letters had succeeded in moulding all his features into the more
bitter and comprehensive sneer.

The day after the *Greenback* arrived in the Slough was publication day at the office of the "Sloughford Weekly Gazette," and, prompted by Madden, Mr Cheevers, the editor, penned a florid and tearful quarter of a column anent the supposed loss of the *Water Nymph*.

"The New Brunswick schooner *Greenback*, commanded and owned by Captain Angus R. Nixon, a gentlemanly and intelligent master-mariner, brings us a piece of intelligence which will cast a gloom over at least two happy homesteads. Captain Nixon picked up in mid-Atlantic a portion of a ship's stern having painted upon it ' Water N ' and ' Slo.' It would be idle, nay, criminal, on our part were we to shut our eyes to the awful gravity which attaches itself to this wooden messenger from the deep. It will be remembered by such of our readers as take an interest in maritime affairs, that the barque *Water Nymph*, commanded by that gallant and daring seaman John M'Cormick, sailed, full of high hope, out of this port on the 15th of March. Since that date no intelligence of the barque has reached Sloughford. Many were of opinion that it was rash of Captain M'Cormick to brave at such a period of the year—when the frozen waters of the north were breaking up, sending across the bosom of the ocean countless masses of drifting ice—the dangers of the sad Atlantic. To be brief, we fear—it has ever been our motto not to mince matters —the ill-fated barque is no more—her last long voyage has terminated. We hope, we earnestly pray, that our conviction may prove an erroneous one, our conclusions hasty and ill-timed ; but, nevertheless, we would say to all—and their name in Sloughford is legion—who take an interest in the fate of the gallant M'Cormick, be prepared for the worst ! We may add —should our surmise prove itself to have been built upon a solid foundation of fact—there is little room for doubt that Captain M'Cormick leaves his (must we say it ?) bereaved widow, and his grief-stricken half-sister comfortably, nay, amply provided for. This should afford them some little consolation in their hour of tribulation. The *Water Nymph,* as is pretty generally known, was the sole property of the brave but ill-starred M'Cormick, and we understand she is fully insured."

. . . .

Richard Dalton walked into Butler's office about eleven o'clock on the day that the " Gazette " announced the supposed loss of the *Water Nymph*. He had come straight from his ship, and had not heard anything of the news brought by the *Greenback*.

Since he had made up his mind to see Mrs M'Cormick never again, he had been quite restless and miserable. In the evenings he usually came on deck, and looking over the bulwarks on the high white poop of the *Atalanta*, his eyes would turn towards the bridge, associated for him with memories of kisses, of vows made but to be broken. Then gradually, dreading lest any one might observe him, he would gaze, full of bitter thoughts, at a white speck visible high up the Bankside slope through the branches of budding trees. He seldom went ashore. He had no desire to renew his acquaintance with any one in Sloughford. His only visitors were Madden and Butler; the former came almost every day on business, the latter two or three times a week to have a chat.

Dalton learned from the shipbroker the history of Sloughford for the years he had been absent, and of the people in whom he once had an interest. He found that nearly all those he had known when a lad had either gone over to the great majority, or had left the ever-changing town. Once he mustered up courage to ask Butler how M'Cormick and his wife got on together—if he thought the latter was happy and contented.

"Happy!" said Butler, somewhat evasively. "Why should she not be happy? She has everything a woman who is not over-ambitious could wish for— a pretty house, plenty of money, and good wishes of everyone that knows her. I grant you," he added, "I could wish, for M'Cormick's sake and for his wife's sake, that Susan Neville had not married a man who has lived the best part of his life in an atmosphere so different from hers, and who is so much older than she is; but one can't have everything in this world. I certainly think she is not deserving of pity, my dear fellow," he continued, seeing that Dalton did not offer to speak. "Of course I know all about the old affair between you both; but you were quite a youngster then, and young men get over these troubles. As for women," he smiled—"well, women easily make up their mind to forget. Are you satisfied now?"

"Oh, Mr Butler," said Dalton, a little uneasily, "you must not think I troubled you with questions about Mrs M'Cormick because I was thinking of what is past and gone for ever. I was anxious to hear from you, who are such an old friend, if M'Cormick treated her well — you know what I mean. Her husband used to be looked upon as a most violent-tempered man. But there, I suppose marriage tones one down. Of course it is no business of mine," he added, as if he were vexed with himself. "But I am so glad to hear she has no cause to be sorry for her bargain."

Butler was on the point of saying he feared she had often cause to regret her act of self-sacrifice, but it struck him it would be highly injudicious to make any such statement to a former lover of Susan, and he wisely held his peace.

.   .   .   .

When Dalton entered Butler's office the day of the announcement in the "Gazette," he was surprised to find the ordinarily placid shipbroker in a state of great excitement.

"This looks like bad news, shocking news; but what a shame it is for the 'Gazette' to put hastily forward the worst side of the case! There is certainly a brighter side. Don't you think so, Dalton?"

" Really I don't know what you are talking about.
What has the ' Gazette '—I should have thought the
old rag had died a natural death long ago—been
doing now to upset you ? "

" Is it possible you have not heard the news ?
Everyone on the quay is discussing it."

" No. I have heard no news this morning that
interests me."

" Not heard about the *Water Nymph ?* "

" What about her ? What is it ? "

Dalton's heart gave a violent throb at the mention
of M'Cormick's ship.

" Read for yourself," handing him a copy of the
" Gazette."

Dalton hastily and excitedly ran his eye through
the paragraph. Then, with beating heart he read
the oddly-worded quarter of a column slowly from
beginning to end. Laying down the newspaper, he
said,—

" I consider that the most stupid and unfair specimen I have seen for many a day, of jumping to
conclusions."

" I am glad indeed that you think so. There is
a glimmer of hope at any rate."

"Of course there is." He tried hard to prevent himself from thinking that possibly there was little hope. "Surely, if a piece of planking is picked up at sea, it does not argue that the ship it may have belonged to has gone down. What the New Brunswicker picked up may not be a portion of the *Water Nymph's* stern at all."

"There is a strong probability, though, that it is.'

"I grant you that. But, supposing the barque is lost, why conclude the crew are lost? It is absurd. It is grossly unfair to shock the feelings of M'Cormick's relatives, by publishing such a piece of rubbish. I wonder some one hasn't gone to the ' Gazette ' office and wrung the editor's neck."

"Oh, you must not be too hard on old Cheevers. He has to make his paper sell."

"It is too bad, too bad," Dalton murmured, his thoughts now far away from Mr Cheevers, and the "Sloughford Gazette." "I hope," he added, after a momentary pause, "she—I mean Mrs M'Cormick—has not seen this," taking up the newspaper again, and glancing through the paragraph.

"I am afraid she has. I believe she takes Mr Cheever's paper. However, I sent Helen—my niece

—over to Bankside immediately after breakfast to break the news to her in case she had not heard it already. I fear Helen was too late. I wish I could have gone over to Woodbine Cottage myself, but I am tied to the office to-day. Madden and Ryan are at the Custom House, and Murphy has gone down the river. Women always say or do something foolish at a time like this. Look here, Dalton, I know you don't care to renew your acquaintance with Susan M'Cormick ; but you might put conventionality aside for to-day, and run across to Bankside."

Dalton who had been standing moodily at the desk bit his lip at the shipbroker's proposal. He would like to go, and yet he felt it would be unwise. He would not care to meet her at such a time, and perhaps she would be displeased if he went. Then he reflected that Miss Cadogan was with Susan, and the presence of a stranger—for he had not attempted to renew his acquaintance with Butler's niece— would prevent any awkwardness from arising. He might be of some real use ; he might be able to make Susan more easy in her mind.

It would be idle to deny that Dalton experienced a wild thrill of hope at the prospect of M'Cormick being no more; but he had the grace to check the feeling instantly, and to despise himself for having entertained it for a moment. Besides, he remembered what Butler had, somewhat untruthfully, told him respecting the relations between Susan and her husband; and in any case, thought Dalton, this piece of news would shock a wife terribly, even supposing she was not violently attached to her husband. And what reason had he to think she did not love him? He had better do as Butler suggested.

Accordingly, giving the shipbroker an assurance that he would endeavour to convince Mrs M'Cormick that there was no need to attach any importance to the surmises of the "Gazette," Dalton set out for Woodbine Cottage.

CHAPTER IV.

DALTON AND MRS M'CORMICK RECEIVE A SHOCK.

IN order to reach Woodbine Cottage, Dalton had to cross the old wooden bridge. As he passed through the gates a dull, depressing feeling, born of memory and disappointed hopes, seized hold of him and saddened him beyond measure. He was now standing upon the spot where Susan and he had lingered, had kissed each other the night before he had left his native town, many years ago. For a moment he stood still.

"I cannot face her," he mused, "and talk platitudes about hope and resignation. What does it matter to me if M'Cormick is no more—what does it matter to me? Oh, no, no, no, a thousand times no! I must not harbour such thoughts," putting out his hands as if to ward off some evil spirit. He walked forward again, endeavouring to think of something, anything, which would take his mind away from the *Water Nymph* and every one connected with her. But the effort was in vain. He found himself constantly wondering could the " Gazette's " surmises be correct ; and, if they were correct, was it possible that after a time Susan would listen to him, would give him some faint hope of future happiness. Did she still care for him ? Sometimes he fancied she did. Sometimes he fancied she did not. But what was the use of all this weighing of impossibilities ? Was it not his intention and desire now to quiet her mind by assurances of the safety of the barque, and how could he hope to simulate a confident tone if he allowed himself to drift into thoughts and indulge in hopes which he felt were, under the circum-stances, unworthy of any honourable man ?

In this unquiet frame of mind he reached the gate of Woodbine Cottage.

As he walked up the gravelled path leading to the house, he was surprised to see Arthur Madden standing at the window. A lady stood alongside

Madden. Dalton had no doubt this was Mrs
M'Cormick, but he kept his eyes fixed on the
ground.

When he entered the sitting-room he found
Madden was alone.

"She has gone away," reflected Dalton sadly.
"She will not see me. Perhaps it is all for
the best."

"I am surprised to find you here, Mr Madden,"
he said, shaking Arthur's hand. "Your governor
told me about an hour ago that you were up to
your eyes in business at the Custom House," seating himself on a low chair near the window.

"So I was. I ought to be there now, I know ;
but I heard some news at the Custom House,
and as I had a punt at the quay, I thought I'd
just pull across to Bankside and tell the good
people here the latest intelligence. Miss Cadogan
was in the room when you opened the gate. She
has gone upstairs to Mrs M'Cormick."

Then it was not Susan he had seen at the window. The discovery caused him to feel, he could
not tell why, strangely happy.

"You said you came here with some news, Mr

Madden. Might I ask what the news is about?
I fancied you were going to tell me."

"Of course I was. The news is about the *Water
Nymph*. What other news could interest Sloughford to-day? We all seem to have *Water Nymph*
on the brain.—Hallo!" he cried, "there's that vessel
tacking again. I must catch her name this time,"
lifting an opera-glass to his eyes, and leaning on
the sill of the half-open window.

What could Madden's news be? Why had he
hesitated to tell him? It was something, perhaps,
which would make him happy or miserable for
ever. Madden must have some important intelligence to relate, or he would not have come across
specially with it. Had the barque arrived safely;
or had her crew been picked up? Or had the
"Gazette's" surmises been confirmed? What did that
fellow at the window mean by his silence? Was
he tantalising him purposely? He dared not show
Madden he was over-anxious to know what the
news was. Madden would perhaps guess the cause
of his anxiety, and he would not wish him to do
so for worlds. And yet why should he not ask
him again? Was not every one curious about

the matter?   Had not Madden himself declared
so a few minutes ago?   He would ask him again.
He could not sit there idly, his fate, it might be,
trembling in the balance.

He moved uneasily in his chair, and looked up
at Madden, who was still at the window, turning
the opera - glass slowly round as if to catch sight
of some moving object.

"Well, well," cried the shipbroker's clerk, almost
flinging the opera-glass from his hand, and turning
round. "This is positively tormenting!"

"What is it?" asked Dalton.

"A vessel is beating up the river, and I just
caught a glimpse of her name, but am not quite
sure of it yet. She's on the other tack now, so
I must wait a bit. I wish there was some regulation to make ships have their names painted on
the bows."

"No doubt if the Board of Trade heard the present regulations were a source of inconvenience or
discomfort to you, they would at once alter the
whole system of navigation," said Dalton, now completely out of temper.

"I didn't know you went in for such sledgehammer sarcasm," rejoined Madden, with a good-humoured laugh. " Do you suffer from liver ? "

Dalton burst into laughter.

" That is the second time to-day that I have been asked about my liver. Have you seen Mrs M'Cormick since you came ? "

" No. Miss Cadogan tells me that she is dread-fully upset at the news; but she promises to come downstairs in a few moments."

" You have some fresh news for her. You said so when I came in. What is it, might I ask ? "

" Oh, yes ! I had almost forgotten. I am rather inclined to look upon it as important too — but I have lost sight of my ship."

" Bother your ship ! "

" If I am right about her, I think, with a little skill, a good sensation poster might be got out by the ' Gazette.' "

" Oh, damn the ' Gazette ! ' "

" What an impatient fellow you are. You would take an interest in the ship, too, if you had only the patience to hear me out—that is, if my eyes did not deceive me a moment ago."

" Why ? What do you mean ? " cried Dalton,

rising from his chair, a vague terror possessing
him.

" Oh, don't look as if you had seen a ghost!
Come here."

Dalton went to the window.

Madden, still holding the opera - glass by his
side, pointed to the river. " Do you see those
ships there ? "

" Yes."

There were some half-dozen vessels, large and
small, beating up the stream with the flood.

" One of them, unless I'm very much mistaken
—there she goes!" he cried, lifting the opera-glass
to his eyes. " Now then," following the movements
of the ship. " Round you go! That's it! Lovely!
.... I'm right," he cried, looking curiously at
Dalton—" *Water Nymph.*"

" *Water Nymph!*" shouted Dalton, seizing the
opera-glass. " The *Water Nymph* in the river again!"

A low cry startled both men. Dalton knew the
cry came from the woman he loved. He turned
swiftly round.

The folding-doors had been opened as Madden
cried out the name of the ship.

CHAPTER V.

IN WHICH THE LANDLADY OF THE " BOLD DRAGOON " COMPETELY LOSES HER TEMPER.

THE next day a woman draped in black toiled up the slope to Woodbine Cottage. Arriving at the door, she knocked loudly, and gave the bell a vigorous tug.

" Is your mistress at home ? " she inquired, as the servant opened the door.

" Yes, ma'am ; but—"

" But what ? Tell her I wish to speak to her. You know me, don't you ? "

" Yes, ma'am."

" Well, don't stand staring at me. Let me pass. I know my way," entering the hall and opening the door of the sitting-room.

The servant mounted the stairs, evidently angered and bewildered.

"The way that girl stared at me — impudent
hussy!" fumed Miss Walsh, seating herself in a
comfortable chair. "One would think I was a
natural curiosity. I hope her mistress will not keep
me waiting long. I wish that stupid man, Madden,
had kept his word, and found out all about John's
will for me—it would have saved me this tiresome
walk. I'll give Mistress Susan a piece of my mind
if she is not straightforward."

Mrs M'Cormick was sitting at the window of her
dressing-room when the servant entered and told
her that Miss Walsh was downstairs. She had not
yet recovered from the excitement and the shock
of the previous day. Her cheeks were deadly white,
and her eyes seemed unnaturally large and dark.

The previous day Madden had reached the house
only a few minutes before Dalton. He was surprised and delighted to find Helen alone in the sitting-room, but he had barely time to say that he
was the bearer of some important news for Mrs
M'Cormick when he saw Dalton approaching the
house. Helen went upstairs when Dalton's knock
was heard at the hall door, and Madden felt he
owed the newcomer a grudge for the interruption,

for he had almost plucked up courage to declare a second time his passion for Helen.

He guessed that the master of the *Atalanta* was still in love with Mrs M'Cormick, and he determined to tantalise him by saying there was further news about the *Water Nymph*, and he would then seek some opportunity of shifting the conversation.

At first he had been staring through the opera-glass simply for the purpose of keeping Dalton in suspense, but he was himself excited when he saw something which looked like *Water Nymph* on the stern of a vessel beating up the river.

"I'll give Dalton a bit of a shock," he thought, " by informing him the *Water Nymph* is in the Slough. It won't be a lie—although it won't be exactly the truth—so he can't kick up a row with me afterwards. If he does, I can assure him I distinctly stated this craft was a brig. What a lark it will be to watch his face when I tell him! I know the fellow would give his eyes to be certain the barque was in Davy's locker."

Susan had seen the statement in the " Sloughford Gazette " before Helen's arrival. Although she had

boasted to her husband that she had no belief in
presentiments, yet she had been indulging in them
for several days, and when she read the newspaper
she had sustained only a dull, stupefying shock.
For some time she had been unaccountably uneasy.
Her husband's words and manner the day she had
last seen him had impressed her strongly, and
filled her with forebodings of evil. The letter
which Dalton had given her, and which she had
read over and over again, as if it had been her
first love-letter, filled her ears with the despairing
cry of a man who knew his end was not far off.
In the letter M'Cormick made but one reference
to the future, and that reference was ominous—
it concerned his will.

When she laid down the "Gazette," she felt assured her husband was no more. For a long time
she sat thinking calmly of her unromantic married
life. One by one all M'Cormick's good qualities
and actions stood out in bold contrast with his
faults and failings. The shadow of death shut out
the ill deeds, and as the shadow faded gradually
his good deeds passed before her mental vision in
glaring colours. Suddenly she burst into a pas-

sionate fit of weeping, disturbed only by Helen's
advent.

They talked together over the news brought by
the *Greenback*, and gradually Mrs M'Cormick experienced a sense of relief. The news might not
be true. Helen's uncle considered no importance
should be attached to it. Perhaps she had been
fretting without cause.

Then Madden's arrival caused a diversion, and soon
afterwards Helen brought Susan word that Dalton
was also below, and that both men wished to see her.

A reaction had now set in. A wild, feverish hope
surged within Susan's breast. She knew she was
wicked beyond measure to indulge in such a hope
even for a moment. But memories of her old, her
only, lover would not be driven out.

She started violently from her chair, a crimson
glow suffusing her cheeks. With a sob in her throat,
she made some inarticulate remark to Helen, and
led her silently down the stairs. She beckoned
Helen to follow her into the sitting-room at the
back, for she could not yet face one of the visitors.
She must first succeed in banishing from her mind
all guilty thoughts of him.

Through the folding-doors she could hear faintly the voices of the men in the outer room. At last she fancied she was prepared to meet her old lover, and she silently opened the folding-door. As she did, she heard Madden's words and Dalton's cry—a cry of wild despair, which she could not restrain herself from echoing; and she remembered nothing more for hours.

When Susan had recovered sufficiently, she learned the truth—at least what Sloughford accepted as the truth—from Helen's lips, namely, that a boat belonging to the *Water Nymph* had been picked up, keel upwards; and there could be now little doubt the barque and all on board had been lost.

A doctor was sent for, and he recommended an immediate change of scene, and suggested a neighbouring watering-place.

Susan had been told she must not for some time see anyone who might excite her or cause her to brood over her husband's death. She knew it was unwise to go down downstairs to Miss Walsh, but she thought she was sufficiently calm to see her, and she felt it might appear unkind if she were to allow her husband's sister to go away without a word sympathy.

When she entered the sitting-room, her visitor's mourning caused Susan to experience a horrible sensation—it brought the fact of M'Cormick's loss home to her in a swift, deadly way. Any lingering doubts she might have entertained were swept away by the crape and bombazine.

Then she found herself wondering how her visitor had managed to deck herself out in mourning so very rapidly. She held out her hand in silence, and she could not repress a shudder as she felt the clasp of Miss Walsh's black-cotton gloved fingers.

"This is terrible news, isn't it ?" said Miss Walsh, lifting her veil. "Poor, dear, John !" She made a desperate but unsuccessful attempt to burst into tears as she spoke.

"Yes," said Susan, sitting down. "But I beseech you not to give way now. Do not let us talk over what has happened. The shock has made me very weak, and I have been forbidden to speak about what has happened, for a little time ; but I could not let you go away without seeing you."

"You are kindness itself," sneered Miss Walsh. "I am not going to distress you by any exhibition of natural grief. Poor, dear John ! It relieves me a

little to give vent to my feelings," patting her eyes
with a black-bordered handkerchief. "There, I'm
better now," with a prolonged snuffle; "and I must
ask you, painful as it is for me to touch upon
such a subject, for some information about my poor
dear brother's worldly affairs."

"Unfortunately, you could not come to a worse
person. At present I am not in a position to give
you any information."

"You decline to do so. Very well, madam, I
must only endeavour to compel you. I came here
with every intention of being reasonable, but allow
me to tell you I am not going to be snubbed by
you or by anyone else."

"It is very wrong to speak to me in that fashion,
Miss Walsh. I have no desire to be uncommuni-
cative, but the fact is, I cannot tell you anything
now. You have no right to distress me. I told
you I was far from being well. Perhaps if you
called on Mr Butler—"

"Rubbish!" interrupted Miss Walsh. "You are
the person to give me the information I require.
You are well aware my brother made a will. Can
you deny that?"

"I don't want to deny or to assert anything, but I must decline to carry on a conversation of this kind."

"Oh! must you, indeed? You know well where the will is, and what is in it to; and you think you can play with me; but I am no child, madam."

"This is very absurd, Miss Walsh. I cannot understand you. Why will you not believe me? It would be of little advantage to hide anything from you—and is it not rather heartless to talk of wills? We cannot be certain of anything yet. We must and we ought to have hope."

"Oh! the barque is lost right enough; and well you know it. There is no use in trying to wriggle out of the truth in that way."

Miss Walsh's brutality aroused whatever was combative in Susan, and disgusted her beyond measure. She had endeavoured to be gentle and forbearing with her visitor, feeling that a sister's grief should be respected, and that the sudden shock had upset Miss Walsh; but it was no longer possible to suppose that her visitor possessed a spark of sisterly feeling, and Susan made up her mind to leave the room without further parley.

Rising, she said, in as quiet a tone as she could command,—

"I do not see that anything but unpleasantness can result by prolonging our conversation."

"Then you absolutely refuse to tell me anything?" cried Miss Walsh furiously, rising with a bound from her chair, an ugly glitter in her stony eyes.

"I have nothing to tell you at present."

"I'll let you see whether you have or not. You want to cheat me out of my rights. That's what you want to do. It's all a game between yourself and your friend Butler, but I'll find a way to make both of you speak."

Susan had now opened the door of the sitting-room.

"Ah! you're running off, are you? All right, my lady," following Susan into the hall, and shouting and shaking her fist as Mrs M'Cormick tremblingly ascended the staircase. "I know all about your goings on lately with young Dalton. I'll make a show of you all over Sloughford. I'll drag your name in the dirt!"

It is impossible to say what further threats Miss Walsh might have delivered herself of had she remained longer at the foot of the stairs, but suddenly she found herself thrust along the hall. Before she could arm herself against an attack, the hall door opened, and with another thrust Miss Walsh was propelled by Mrs M‘Cormick's muscular maid into the outer air.

CHAPTER VI.

NIXON FINDS HIMSELF IN STRANGE COMPANY,
AND BEHOLDS HIS FATE.

THE *Greenback* was not ordered into a discharging berth until the second day after her arrival in the Slough.

The master of the schooner was exceedingly wroth when he discovered that Madden had befooled him about Thornhill. However, the ship-broker's clerk was confident he knew the temperament the man with whom he had to deal, and when he saw the *Greenback* alongside the wharf, he went on board with a swaggering gait and a jaunty air.

He demonstrated to Nixon the unwisdom of making a row: such a course, he argued, could not mend matters, and every one in Sloughford would only laugh at the manner in which the stranger had been taken in, if the story once became public property.

"If you cannot make up your mind to forgive me," Madden went on volubly, "there is nothing for it but to hand over your ship's papers to Thornhill—of course we would not dream of detaining them in our office against your will. After all, you will find we can do as well for your interest as anyone else, and I shall take care that the little subterfuge of mine shall be a strict secret between ourselves. You must admit, Captain Nixon, that competition is so keen in these days a man should have his wits about him and be up to all sorts of tricks and dodges in order to do any good. Moreover you are not the injured party— if anybody is really injured—in this case. Thornhill is the man who would have the most cause for complaint, but he need never be the wiser if we both agree, like sensible men, to hold our tongues."

After some deliberation, Nixon decided upon accepting Madden's view of the situation.

"Waal, let it be! I'll forgive your little trick, if I can't forget it. You were a size too sharp

for me the day afore yesterday; but I wasn't prepared for falling foul in this forgotten corner of
the globe of any but the most dead-and-alive set
of sogers. I was off my guard, I was, and that
is how you got to win'ard of me so mighty easy.
But don't you go calculating, young man, you're
going to find a softy again in Angus R. Nixon.
If you do, you'll discover yourself a long way to
leeward in your calculations."

"Oh, Captain Nixon, I'd want to be a thorough
stupid if I did not know I was dealing with a
man whose head is as hard as hickory. But even
Solomon himself, and those daring seafarers, the wise
men of Gotham, were sometimes caught napping."

Nixon was flattered at being compared with
Solomon and with any collection of wise men. He
had never heard of the Gotham wiseacres, but as
Madden declared they were seafarers, he felt there
was a professional as well as a mental relationship
existing between them and him.

"I rather like you, young man," said the skipper, after making up his mind he would allow
the *Greenback's* papers to remain in Butler's hands.
"It ain't often I takes a fancy to new hands, but

your headpiece seems to be screwed on pretty tight, it do; and that's what suits me down to the ground. You understand me, don't you?"

"Perfectly. It is a case of the sympathy which naturally exists between two great minds. Look us up at the office during the day. If you like, I'll show you round the town this evening as soon as I get done with my work. By the way, your log-book seems to be rather in a mess. You have scarcely made an entry in it."

"No. That's what fixes me; but keep it dark. I'm rather backward at that sort of work, somehow. What's to be done?"

"It would have been a very simple matter, but for the wreckage you picked up. There will be some sort of inquiry over the loss of the *Water Nymph*, so we shall have to be cautious. We must have an hour or so together this evening. Your ship ought to have been reported by this time; but as you haven't started at discharging, I suppose it won't make much difference."

"Yes. The officer in charge here told me I'd get into a row over it."

"Oh, we'll make it all square? I'll get the log-

book to rights before morning. I'll doctor it. I
rather like that kind of work; it gives such play
to the imagination."

"Risky game, ain't it?"

"Sometimes. I was very near getting into
trouble last week. A fat, unromantic Welshman
hadn't made an entry in his log from start to finish, and he was so infernally stupid I could get
nothing out of him in the shape of information, so
I had to work the whole voyage out myself."

"And, of course, you made a mess of it."

"Of course I didn't. But I chased that craft
with an albatross for weeks, and introduced bits
of the 'Ancient Mariner' here and there. The collector of customs happened to look through the
log, and he thought he had got hold of a salt-water
Shakespeare, so he asked the old skipper to dinner.
I heard it was about the most amusing thing on
record—the collector trying to draw out the liter-
ary skipper, and the poor old skipper thinking the
collector was a raving lunatic. But," observing
that Nixon did not enjoy the joke, "I am wasting
your valuable time, Captain Nixon, and my own,
too, I fear. I'll say bye-bye for the present."

The master of the *Greenback* lounged into Butler's office during the afternoon, and was conducted by Foxy Ned into Ryan's office.

"Mr Madden and the governor are inside, captain," said Ned, pointing to the office to the left of the passage, "so you'd better take a seat in here for the present. Mr Michael"—to Ryan,—"this is the captain of the *Greenback*."

About half-a-dozen skippers were seated round the fire. Amongst them were the Bishop, whose ship was going to sail in the morning; Bendall, whose ship was still under repair; and Carmody, who was in extra ill-humour—his craft was taking in a cargo of oats, and was being delayed an unreasonably long time. Captains Cummins, Broaders, and Sullivan had gone to sea during the previous week; and Captain Arkwright was probably slumbering in the "Nest."

After exchanging a few words with Ryan, who was still nervous about facing the New Brunswicker, the master of the *Greenback* took a chair and joined in the conversation going on among the skippers.

"You are the gentleman, I believe," said the

Bishop, "who was the first bearer of the sad news about the *Water Nymph*."

"Yes. Did you know the master?"

"Know him! Ah, indeed I did, captain. I can remember the time when we were gay, heedless youngsters, playing leap-frog and pegging tops together."

Bendall laughed loudly.

"What ails you, Tom Bendall? It's very ignorant, I can tell you, and moreover very unseemly, to be grinning away there when people are talking of such serious matters."

"Oh, dear! oh, dear!" chuckled Bendall. "I was just picturing you, Captain Augy, playing leap-frog with your top hat planted well over your ears, and pegging a top with your umbrella made fast under your arm."

Carmody, who had been indulging in a fit of silent anger, laughed a short, rasping laugh, which seemed to irritate the Bishop even more than Bendall's interruption.

"It's disgusting, fairly disgusting!" said the Bishop, wheeling round his chair and turning his back on Carmody.

'Don't you take on so," said Nixon. "You was

going to say something to me, I think, when these gentlemen here interrupted you."

"Yes, captain. I was going to ask your opinion about the *Water Nymph*. It seems a vessel has arrived in Liverpool which picked up one of the barque's boats, bottom up. I suppose you have heard this already?"

"No; indeed I have not. I have only just come ashore."

"Mr Madden—Mr Butler's clerk—heard so at the Custom House, so I suppose there can be little doubt now as to John M'Cormick. What's your opinion, Captain Nixon?"

"Waal, my opinion is easily given, stranger. Your friend's ship is at the bottom of the Atlantic, and so is every man Jack of her crew. I said so to Mr Madden the day I arrived in the river, and when I says a thing straight, I aint generally far astray."

"Sad! Terribly sad!" murmured the Bishop. "Well, well, it may be all our fate one of these fine days," shaking his head solemnly.

"Those that are born to be hanged needn't have much to fear of drowning," smiled Carmody.

"A very ignorant and a very foolish remark, Pat. I wonder at you," droned the Bishop.

"How curious it was," said Bendall, "that a vessel of the same name should have arrived at the quay yesterday!"

"Is that so?" said Nixon. "Yes, it is a bit curious. A barque?"

"No, a brig."

"What's curious about it?" snarled Carmody. "I never heard such a parcel of nonsense. Curious! I suppose there are forty ships of the same name knocking about. It's mighty easy to amuse you all. Curious! Faugh!"

"I hope you're getting on faster with the loading, Pat?" said the Bishop soothingly, turning round and facing Carmody again. "Did you get much oats on board yesterday?"

"Not as much as would make a meal for a genet. 'Tis enough to put a man in a fair rage."

Butler and Madden now entered Ryan's office. Madden shook hands with Nixon cordially, and turning to the shipbroker, said,—

"This is the master of the New Brunswick schooner."

"Welcome to Sloughford!" said Butler, "although you haven't been the bearer of good news. Mr Madden and I were speaking about you a few minutes ago."

" Nothing bad, I hope," smiled Nixon.

" No. We were discussing the loss of the barque whose wreckage you fell in with. It seemed strange to me at first that her stern had been torn away if she ran into the ice."

" Easily explained, sir. No manner of doubt 'twas owing to a bad look-out, and very likely the disaster came off in the night time. I reckon there was a heap of confusion on board, and some one brought her round with a crash, stern on to the ice. That's how I reckon it was, and Angus R. Nixon—that's me, Mr Butler—ain't often far astray in his reckonings. I said as much the first time your clerk came aboard my little craft."

" Evidently the poor fellows are all lost," sighed the shipbroker. " I suppose there was no time to launch the boats. It's a sad affair. It has quite upset me."

" Ay, indeed!" murmured the Bishop. " Poor John M'Cormick! He looked so full of life and hope the last time we saw him in the office here, sir. Ah, the sea is a poor profession! It's only fit for dogs, or the very dregs of humanity."

"Was there anything found in the boat the Liverpool ship picked up?" asked Bendall.

"Was there anything found in the boat!" sneered Carmody. "Was there anything found in a boat picked up bottom upwards? Did any man ever hear such a question? I suppose there was nothing more in her than is in your head this minute, Tom Bendall —emptiness."

"Pat, Pat," cried the Bishop, shaking his forefinger at Carmody, "is there any use in my talking to you at all? Fie! fie! Pat." Then turning to the ship-broker,—"I wonder, sir, did poor John perish well off?"

"I don't know; but I fancy he made a good deal of money latterly. Sometimes I have hopes we shall, in spite of everything, hear something more of M'Cormick."

"Never!" said Nixon emphatically.

"May I ask, captain," inquired Carmody, "where, how, and when you obtained the gift of prophecy?"

"I don't understand you, sir."

"It isn't to be expected you could understand Pat Carmody all in a minute," said the Bishop apologetically. "You mustn't heed him, Captain Nixon. He's a well-meaning man, but very hasty in his remarks."

"I don't want a character from you, at any rate, Augy Flynn," cried Carmody, with blazing eyes.

"Oh, dear! oh, dear!" chuckled Bendall.

Butler for some minutes had been paying little or no attention to the conversation of the skippers. He stood with his back against the mantelpiece, thinking how he ought to act with regard to M'Cormick's will. If M'Cormick was dead, he ought to produce the will at once; and yet he could not divest himself of a lingering doubt as to the fate of the *Water Nymph*. If M'Cormick was still in the land of the living, it would be better to make no mention of the tin case now lying in the safe, for the will in his possession might not be M'Cormick's last will. Mrs M'Cormick had not, on her husband's own admission, been treated fairly, and the master of the *Water Nymph* had promised faithfully to reconsider the matter. Husband and wife had, he knew, parted on much better terms than usual. If he gave up the will, some effort would probably be made by those whom the will might benefit to establish the fact of the loss of the barque. This would be sure to upset Mrs M'Cormick, and in her present state of health any unusual excitement or worry might be a serious injury to her.

His reveries and the conversation of the skippers were suddenly interrupted by the entrance of a lady dressed in black.

" I want a word with you at once, Mr Butler," said the lady, lifting her veil. " Can we have a few minutes together ? "

" Certainly," said Butler. " If you will come with me into the other office we can talk there."

The features of this lady were unfamiliar to the master of the. *Greenbuck*, but he felt a fluttering at his heart as he, in company with the other mariners, sat staring at Miss Walsh.

After the landlady of the " Bold Dragoon " had left Ryan's office with Butler, the Bishop informed Nixon that the visitor was John M'Cormick's half-sister. The New Brunswicker also learned that she was unmarried and had expectations.

" The very thing for me," he thought. " Women folk never seemed to interest me before ; but this party, I reckon, would just about suit me."

It would be impossible to discover any element of beauty or grace in Miss Walsh's features. The lines were hard, determined, and angular, and there was a certain air of masculinity in her appearance which repelled most men. Perhaps it was this very masculinity which attracted the skipper of the *Greenback*. If he had met the lady for the first time behind the counter of the "Bold Dragoon," he would not, in all probability, have devoted a second thought to the consideration of her charms; but her dramatic entrance, and .the defiant manner she had adopted when addressing the shipbroker, made their mark on the ordinarily unimpressionable "Blue Nose."

"A woman like that," he mused, "knows her way about, you may bet. No nonsense there. None of your whining, whimpering, good-for-nothing baby faces, that raddles their jaws and coaltars their eyebrows, and has as much false hair in their clothes-chest as would make a shore mooring for a full-rigged ship. I'd best make a move in that direction, I had."

Accordingly he bade good-bye to his companions, and told Madden, who was busy writing at Ryan's

desk, that he would return to the office in the course
of an hour.

Miss Walsh was still in Madden's office with the
shipbroker, but Nixon made up his mind she would
not remain there very long.

"Women of that sort don't lose no unnecessary
time," he argued. "She'll be back to headquarters
before many more minutes are over."

As he came into the passage he saw Foxy Ned
— a scrubby-faced, shabbily-dressed little man —
leaning, in a reverie, against the jamb of the
office door. He tapped Ned on the shoulder, and
asked which was the way to the "Bold Dragoon."

"I'll show you the road with pleasure, captain,"
said Ned briskly, rosy visions of gratuitous drinks
filling all the odd corners of his mind.

"I can find my way without a bodyguard. Just
you direct me straight, my red-headed filibuster.
I know the sort of games you like to play, better
than you can tell me. You chaps have as keen
a scent for cheap drinks as a red Injun, you
have ; but you aint going to come the soger over
Angus R. Nixon — that's me, whisky face. You
tell me the shortest cut right straight away, that's

what you'll do; or I'll be having a little talk with your master."

With a half-suppressed growl, Foxy Ned told Nixon where the "Bold Dragoon" was situated.

"You think yourself mighty clever, don't you, Misther Blue Nose?" growled Ned, as Nixon walked away. "But if I don't make the loss of that drink cost you a sight more than a barrel of beer, you insultin' vagabone, may I never put a pewther measure to my lips again. I'll lead you the life of a dog, believe me, while you're in this port anyhow; or my name isn't Edward Murphy!"

CHAPTER VII.

AT THE SHIPBROKER'S HOUSE.

DALTON had now little, if any, doubt as to the fate of M'Cormick. He was convinced the *Water Nymph* had been lost with all hands. Still, he knew that nothing could be proved satisfactorily, and it was useless for him to indulge in foolish dreams.

His ship was discharging very slowly, and probably a fortnight would elapse before the last of the cargo would be taken away. He now felt wretched as he thought of the delay. He was anxious to leave Sloughford at once. He dared not trust himself to meet Susan, with the knowledge that her husband, in all probability, no longer stood between them.

Did Susan care for him ? and if she did, would it not be all the better they did not see each other for a long time ? How long ? It must be years. Marriage she could not think of so long as there was no absolute certainty with regard to M'Cormick's fate. Why should he dream of marriage ? It was absurd. Susan had most likely ceased long ago to care for him. Had she ever cared for him ? If she had, could she not have waited ?

He was constantly tortured with conflicting thoughts. At one time he fancied Susan had never ceased to remember him, and would perhaps listen to him again if she were convinced she was free. Then he reflected that his long absence, the great change Susan had passed through—the life she had led for the years she was the wife of M'Cormick, the new ties and duties she had taken upon herself—must have blotted him effectually from her heart. Had her heart been ever his ? Never ! She was like all other women, fickle, deceitful. And if she did, after a lapse of years, consent to listen to a renewal of his declaration of love, might not M'Cormick return ?— such things had happened often before—and then for a second time the cup of happiness would be dashed from his lips. He must trample his hopes and desires under foot once more.

Towards evening he came ashore, and walked to Butler's office. He found the shipbroker alone in Madden's office.

"I am glad you looked me up this evening, Dalton," said Butler. "I should like to have a long chat with you. I am troubled very much, and perhaps you could help me out of my difficulty."

"I shall be only too pleased if I can be any assistance to you. You seem rather out of sorts."

"Yes. I had a most unpleasant quarter of an hour to-day—but this isn't a very comfortable place to indulge in a confidential chat. You had best come home with me and have a cup of tea. I don't think you have met my niece since your arrival here. Too bad of you to make such a stranger of yourself."

"I met Miss Cadogan yesterday at Woodbine Cottage."

"Of course. I had forgotten. She told me all about it. Mrs M'Cormick is sadly upset, I fear. She is going out of the town."

"Going out of town! Where?"

"Not very far. To Rosspoint. The doctor said she had better get away from Sloughford at once, and

Rosspoint is very quiet just now. But we had better make a start before anyone comes to detain me here. I can hear Captain Carmody in Ryan's office now. What a shrill voice he has! It goes through me like a knife."

Butler and Dalton left the office, and were soon seated in the shipbroker's drawing-room.

Helen made no reference to the scene at Wood-bine Cottage. She had learned one secret, namely, that Susan was in love with Dalton. Her woman's instinct divined at once the cause of Susan's cry.

After tea, the two men settled themselves down for a chat; and Helen, at her uncle's request, seated herself at the piano.

" I am going to tell you a bit of a secret, at least what I considered a secret until to-day," began Butler, leaning back in his armchair and folding his arms. " And I am then going to ask your advice."

" I am too inexperienced, I fear, to advise anyone," smiled Dalton.

" Well, let me be the judge of that. Now, to begin at the beginning. The evening before the *Water Nymph* sailed from Sloughford, John M'Cormick came to my office and left in my care his will.

. . . Helen," he said, turning his face towards his niece, "play 'The Last Glimpse of Erin' for us."

Dalton was glad the shipbroker had turned his head away, even for a moment. The mere mention of the *Water Nymph* made him experience a momentary sensation of mingled curiosity and uneasiness. "Isn't that the 'Coulin' Miss Cadogan is playing?" he inquired, as the shipbroker again turned his face towards Dalton.

"Yes. It is the same air—the 'Coulin' and 'The Last Glimpse of Erin.'"

"How strange," said Dalton, "that you should have asked Miss Cadogan to play 'The Last Glimpse of Erin' just after speaking of M'Cormick and his ship!"

"I never thought of that," said the shipowner, drawing his eyebrows together. "It is odd. The air is an especial favourite of mine, particularly when I am not in a very bright humour; it's melancholy, strange to say, has a soothing effect upon me. But to go back to the *Water Nymph.* M'Cormick left me his will, with a strict injunction not to tell anyone I had the document. He assured me no one except himself and the man who drafted the will knew of its existence—how other people managed to find out that such a document existed puzzles me—and as he had not treated his wife well in it, he promised to make a new will when he returned from Quebec."

"What a pity he did not destroy the will before he sailed, if he felt uneasy about its contents!"

"Yes. It was a pity. I strongly advised him to do so. But he was a strange, incomprehensible man. I never could understand him. Well, judge of my astonishment when his half-sister called on me to-day and insisted upon my producing her brother's will. I could not tell her a lie when she asked me point-blank if I had the document in my possession."

"I suppose there is no reasonable room for doubt that M'Cormick is no more."

"None now, I should say. I am quite puzzled how I ought to act. I promised M'Cormick I would not let anyone see his will. He may possibly, not probably I own, be still alive; and if so, I have no right to break my promise to him. I thought I would ask some one's advice, and you came into the office just as I had arrived at that determination. Two heads, you know, are better than one."

" I confess I am in a puzzle what to say. I suppose it would be best to give up the will to Mrs M'Cormick. She is the proper person to decide whether its contents should be made known at present or not. At least that is my opinion."

" I think that is an admirable suggestion, Dalton."

The last strains of the " Coulin " had now died away. Turning towards Helen, her uncle said,—" You might sing it for us now, dear—that is, if Captain Dalton is not tired of it."

"Tired of it!" exclaimed Dalton. " Certainly not. Do, please, Miss Cadogan, sing it. It is such a long time since I ever heard any music. I haven't heard the ' Coulin ' for—well, for more years than I should like to mention."

Helen, who had overheard some of the conversation about the *Water Nymph*, experienced an unaccountable depression while she had been playing. The sadness of the melody usually had little effect upon her—custom had made her callous to it. With a smile, however, she nodded to Dalton, and took a volume of songs from the music waggon at her side.

" I thought I heard a tap at the door," said Butler, in an undertone, looking at Dalton.

"So did I."

Butler rose, and advancing noiselessly across the carpet, opened the door,

Helen's clear voice rang out,—

"*Though the last glimpse of Erin with sorrow I see*," as the door was opened wide.

A servant appeared at the doorway, and said, "Mrs M'Cormick, if you please, sir."

Susan, who had heard the words of the song, and whose thoughts instantly flew back to the day she had said good-bye to her husband in the cabin of the *Water Nymph*, tottered into the room.

Butler started forward and placed his arm round Mrs M'Cormick. Almost immediately she recovered, a delicate pink flush stealing into her cheeks.

"Thank you, Mr Butler," she said. "I had no right, I suppose, to tax my strength by such a long walk."

Helen was now at her side, and led her to a chair. Dalton, who had risen from his chair in alarm as he beheld Mrs M'Cormick enter the room, shook hands with her, and went back to his seat.

"It was indeed very wrong of you," said Butler,

"to overtax your strength — I presume you have walked from Bankside ? "

"Yes," she smiled. " But don't make me feel uncomfortable by reminding me of my misdeeds. I am all right now. I was very anxious to see you, Mr Butler ; and you know, I suppose, that I am going out of town to-morrow."

" Why did you not send for me ? "

" I did not want to give you so much trouble. I have been always too great a trouble to you, I fear."

Butler shook his head.

" Perhaps you will excuse me for saying ' Good evening ? ' " said Dalton, standing up. " I suppose," addressing himself to Susan, " I must bid you good-bye, Mrs M'Cormick. We are not likely to meet again."

Butler looked inquiringly at Mrs M'Cormick.

" Please don't go, Captain Dalton," she said, a little uneasily. " What I have to say to Mr Butler will not occupy many minutes. I fear I have interrupted him and you by coming in."

" N—no. Not at all," stammered Butler.

" Yes ; I know I did. Helen and I will run off

together for a few minutes, and let you finish your conversation. Come, Helen," she said, rising and placing her arm round Helen's waist.

"We shall give you just ten minutes, uncle."

"Very well," said Butler, opening the door. "How ill that woman looks, Dalton," he frowned, coming back to his chair.

"Yes. I wonder could anything particular have disturbed her mind to-day?"

"I cannot tell. Stop!" he cried. "I know what it is—at least I fancy I do."

"No further news about her husband's ship?"

"No. I am sure that virago, Miss Walsh, has been paying her a visit. I was on the point of putting the question to that charmingly offensive lady in the office to-day, but something drove it out of my head. That must be it. No doubt she has been tormenting Mrs M'Cormick about the will."

"You told me that M'Cormick assured you no one knew of its existence?"

"So he said; but he was such an absent-minded man at times, and so fond of letting his tongue run away with him, that he may have told his sister. Besides, the will which I hold was drawn up by somebody; and, of course, whoever did draft it knows its contents."

"I am sure, then, the best thing for you to do is to take legal advice upon the matter, and find out some means of saving Mrs M'Cormick from persecution."

"I will do so to-morrow. Here are the ladies," he said, rising as a tap was heard at the door.

Mrs M'Cormick and Helen entered the room.

"Well, uncle," inquired Helen, "have you both said all you have to say to each other?"

"Not all; but for the present we are finished."

"Then, Captain Dalton, I'll ask you to accompany me to the piano, and turn over some music for me, while Mrs M'Cormick and my uncle have a little chat. We are all determined to be brimful of business and mysterious consultations this evening."

Dalton and Helen crossed to the other end of the room. Mrs M'Cormick sat down near Butler. He drew his chair close to hers.

"Now, Captain Dalton, what shall I play for you?" asked Helen, stooping and turning over some music in the waggon.

"Anything you please. Only let it be lively this
time. I am quite low-spirited. That melancholy
'Coulin' has not died out of my ears yet."

Helen looked up at him, and smiled.

"I wish uncle was not so fond of melancholy
airs," she said. Then, in an undertone, "And I
wish somebody would endeavour to silence Miss
Walsh, or at least discover some means for keeping
her away from Mrs M'Cormick. She has almost
worried her out of her wits."

Dalton drew his eyebrows together. Butler was
right in his surmise.

"To-day!"

Helen nodded; and rising, said,—

"Now, I think I have something that ought to
please you, although I know it is very wicked to
indulge in anything lively at such a time as this.
However, Mrs M'Cormick will know, I am sure, that
it isn't from want of sympathy," and, seating herself
at the piano, she commenced to play an arrangement
of Irish dance music.

Dalton, with half-averted glance, was looking at
Susan, and wondering what she had to say to the
shipbroker. He could see they were both deeply

interested in their conversation. He had forgotten his duties at the piano, when Helen's "Turn over, please," caused him to start.

"I am afraid," murmured Helen, as he fumbled over the leaves of the music, "you take more interest in somebody than in my poor music."

He coloured and stammered an apology. In a few moments he found himself again glancing towards Susan. What was she handing Butler? It must be —yes, it was—the very letter which he had given to her the day he arrived in Sloughford. Butler was placing it in his pocket without reading it. No doubt the letter contained something which required his consideration.

The music had now ceased. Mrs M'Cormick turned and said,—

"I am afraid I have been very rude, Helen; and I am afraid I am going to be still more rude to Captain Dalton, for I am going to take you away from the piano. I must get home at once."

Dalton felt a thrill of delight at the prospect of escorting Susan to Woodbine Cottage. Already an ill-defined project to stand with Susan on the bridge, in the place where they had kissed each other years ago, and to discover if her heart was still his own, floated through his mind.

" May I have the pleasure of seeing you home, Mrs M'Cormick ? " he said shyly.

" No, no," she replied. " I don't want any escort. Thank you very much, Captain Dalton ; but really I would prefer to go home alone. You see I am determined to be rude this evening."

" Go home alone ! " said Butler, rising from his chair. " Indeed, you shall do nothing of the sort. Come, Helen, get on your things."

" Really, Mr Butler," began Susan.

" The question admits of no argument," he interrupted, with a wave of his hand. " Helen and I require a walk badly ; it is purely a piece of selfishness on our part."

" Be it so then. It is too bad of me to be such a trouble to you."

" Now, you ladies had better be off to your room. You will come over to Bankside with us, Dalton, won't you ? "

A slight flush came into Susan's cheeks as the shipbroker asked the question. She had an instinctive dread of crossing the bridge in company with her old lover, even if he and she were not alone.

Dalton stammered an apology. He thought he had better get back to his ship; it had just occurred to him that he had some accounts to go through.

"Nonsense!" said Butler. "You will come, of course, I want most particularly to have a chat with you."

CHAPTER VIII.

IN WHICH THE SHIPBROKER RELATES A STORY.

FTER leaving the house, Helen and Susan went forward, arm in arm, followed by Butler and Dalton.

For some time the shipbroker was silent; then, turning to his companion, he said, somewhat abruptly,—

"Will you promise not to be offended with me if I speak to you on a subject which concerns you very closely, and which you may think should not concern me in the least?"

Dalton guessed what the subject was, and in a nervous, agitated manner answered,—

"I promise you not to be offended at anything you may say. I know well you would not speak to me unless you had an excellent reason for doing so."

"Thank you. I fear I am going to tread on very

delicate ground, and there is nothing I abhor more than meddling in matters which do not concern me; but in this case I feel I have a duty to perform."

" Please, then, don't hesitate to speak to me."

" Well, to be quite candid with you, I fancy you remember only too well the relations which long ago existed between you and Susan M'Cormick. Don't answer me if you don't wish to do so. If you can tell me you look upon her merely as a friend, that love has no place in your regard for her, then I need not trouble you by making any further reference to the subject, and can only say I am sorry for what I have said."

Dalton paused. He could not exactly understand what Butler meant by questioning him about his love for Susan. Could Butler have learned any further news about M'Cormick? He was almost afraid to ask. Should he be perfectly candid with the shipbroker? What could he gain by being uncandid?

" I cannot truthfully declare that love has no place in my regard for Mrs M'Cormick," he said, in a low tone. Then lifting his head, and speaking almost defiantly, " I cannot help myself. I know it is foolish—wicked, if you will, but I love her. She is never out of my thoughts. You cannot convince me more strongly than I can convince myself of the folly and the danger of my passion ; but I shall take care it brings injury to no one except myself."

" You are excited now, Dalton ; I did not mean to excite you. I want you to listen to me calmly."

" It is very silly of me," said Dalton apologetically, " to play the part of broken-hearted lover to you."

" I do not see anything silly in your admission ; I see only the danger that may result."

" How ? You surely do not think I would tell Mrs M'Cormick what I have told you now ? "

" You may be sorely tempted. Don't be frightened, Dalton ; I am not going to preach you a sermon."

" You misjudge me altogether."

" No. You misjudge yourself. Besides, there is another side to the question."

" What is the other side ? "

" Ah ! " said Butler, shaking his head, " I cannot give the other side of the question ; I only draw my own conclusions ; and we are all liable to make mistakes."

Dalton was mystified. The shipbroker and he had

now reached the bridge gate. Helen and Susan were standing at the gate.

"We thought we had lost you altogether," said the former. "Mrs M'Cormick insists that we have come quite far enough with her, and wants us to turn back."

"Nonsense," said Butler. "Captain Dalton and I are enjoying the walk immensely, and it would be quite a shame if Mrs M'Cormick were to send us back now. Can't you and she find anything to talk about, Helen?"

"Oh, indeed we can, uncle. I suppose the fact is she is worried by my chatter."

"To prove distinctly that I am not, I shall now insist upon your accompanying me to the very door of my house, and then I shall inveigle you inside, as a punishment for your persistency. If the walk up the hill causes you to feel worn out to-morrow you will have only yourself to blame, Helen."

The two women walked briskly forward, Butler and Dalton following slowly.

"I am delighted to see Mrs M'Cormick in better spirits. There was quite a colour in her cheeks as she spoke," said the shipbroker.

"Yes," said Dalton, a little sadly.

He had noticed that Susan had not once looked in his direction as they stood at the gate.

" Now, Dalton, I must tell you what I wished to say to you to-night. You are in love with Mrs M'Cormick. Let it be granted that she is not aware of the fact, and that you will leave Sloughford shortly without uttering one word of love in her presence. But you do not know the measure of your own strength or your own weakness. You will, I am sure, do all in your power to act rightly, to live down the love which possesses you. You will go away from Sloughford, perhaps, with the determination of never coming back to it. But remember you made up your mind long ago to forget her, and you found yourself unable to do so. After many years, you acknowledge you admire her as much as ever."

" As much! A thousand times more, if that were possible."

" Very well. The same thing will happen again. You will find an attraction here which drags you irresistibly to her side, and then, if she listens to you—"

" If she only would."

" There! You see I told you I knew the strength

and weakness of your character better than you did yourself."

"I did not mean what I said just now. I would not dare to talk of love to her."

"I don't know. I should not care to answer for you. Perhaps it may seem strange to you that I should speak to you as I have spoken to-night, but I know—believe me when I say I know—the terrible danger of your position and hers, should both of you ever forget your duty. I dread what might possibly happen, more than words could tell. Listen to me. I will tell you a story—I can vouch for the truth of every word of it, strange and improbable as it may appear. When you hear it, you will see the danger in a clearer light than you have ever seen it before, and you will know why I am so much in earnest to-night."

There was a wild, haggard expression on Butler's face, which impressed Dalton even more than the earnestness of the shipbroker's speech. Although the night air was cool, large drops of sweat trickled down Butler's cheeks. He lifted his hat, and taking his handkerchief from his pocket, wiped his brow.

"You are distressing yourself, Mr Butler," said

Dalton. "It is too bad that I should be the cause of so much trouble to you."

A tender smile flitted across Butler's face.

"I am afraid I am thinking more of Susan than of you. I have learned to look upon her almost as a daughter. Now for my story. A friend of mine, a young man—younger than you, Dalton—lived within easy distance of a large seaport—not Sloughford, I may tell you. He was fond of ships, and was in the habit of visiting the seaport as often as he conveniently could. His father was at the time moderately wealthy, and had a strong desire that his son should make a good match. The son was, I am afraid, rather a harum-scarum young fellow, and his father, who was stern and reserved, had often warned him that he would disown him if he ever formed a connection without obtaining his consent. During one of the young man's visits to the seaport which I spoke of he fell in love at first sight—such things do happen, I believe—with a very pretty girl. He learned that the girl had married, about a twelvemonth previously, the master of a ship trading out of the port. Her husband was a brute—a coarse, unsympathetic, jealous man, who bullied and beat her before they had

been married two months. Shortly before my friend
saw this young girl for the first time, a rumour reached
the port that the husband's ship had foundered at sea,
and that all hands had perished. The rumour was
afterwards confirmed; but just as in the case of the
Water Nymph, there was no absolute proof that the
crew had gone down with the ship. To cut the matter
short, my friend and the supposed widow fell mutu-
ally in love. The former knew that his father would
not for a moment listen to his son's forming a connection with the widow of a merchant captain. The
young people were both very fond and very foolish,
and decided upon living together secretly, the young
man promising, and fully intending, to marry the
woman as soon as positive proof could be obtained
of the loss of her husband. The great dread which
the woman experienced was the dread that her husband might one day return to claim her, and if he
heard that she had been unfaithful, she had no doubt
he would stop short at nothing—not even murder itself. However, her lover, with great difficulty, succeeded in inducing her to go away with him. She
had no relatives in the seaport, and she told those
who knew her that she intended living with some

friends in another part of the country. She quitted the seaport, leaving behind her no suspicion of her real intentions. Some time afterwards a son was born, and when the boy was about two years of age, a strange and startling rumour reached the young people's ears—"

"The husband was alive!" interrupted Dalton excitedly.

"Yes. Fortunately the connection has been kept a strict secret. My friend's father never suspected his son had disobeyed him, and the people in the seaport had almost forgotten the existence of the woman. The husband was alive, and was on his way back to the seaport. My friend was almost frantic with despair. He knew he had no claim to another man's wife, and the woman's fears of violence on her husband's part came back to her with fourfold strength. He would follow her to whatever part of the earth she might fly. There was nothing for it but to go back to the seaport to await her husband's coming. She did so; it was like going back to the grave. But what could she do? what could her lover do? She succeeded in allaying her husband's suspicions. He did suspect something had gone wrong during his absence, but he was, after a fashion, fond of his wife— about the only good quality in his coarse nature— and he was, I suppose, anxious to deceive himself into the belief that the account which she gave of herself was correct. At all events, husband and wife are still, I believe, living together. My friend never saw the woman he loved with all his heart and soul since the day they parted years and years ago. Their son does not know who his parents are. My friend's life has been utterly spoiled. He is—I have it from his own lips—as much in love to-day with the woman he would have married, as he was when they first met. The man —he is getting old and grey now—dare not tell the secret to his own son. If he did so, the son might possibly let the secret slip from him. And one of the greatest troubles the father has to endure is to see his son drifting into frivolous, perhaps evil ways, without being able to hold out the strong arm of a parent, and snatch him back. Is not that a strange and a dreadful story of spoilt lives, Dalton?"

"It seems almost incredible."

" I told you I could vouch for the truth of every word of it."

" And is the secret known to no one except your friend and the woman he loved, and to yourself ? "

" To those alone.   Now, do you wonder, Dalton, that I have a horror of anything occurring between you and Susan M'Cormick ? "

" I do not indeed," cried Dalton, seizing Butler's hand, " and I shall take warning.   Thank you, my best of friends, for your story."

A heavy tear-drop fell on Dalton's hand. He looked swiftly at the shipbroker's face.   The tears were coursing down his cheeks.

CHAPTER IX.

IN WHICH DALTON BREAKS A GOOD RESOLUTION.

THE two men walked on in silence. At first Dalton was under the impression that the shipbroker's story was an invention—a forecast of what might happen should he forget the peculiar position which Susan held—neither a wife nor a widow. It was almost incredible that a case bearing such a strong resemblance to his own should have occurred within the experience of his friend. But the shipbroker's earnestness, and the pathos which found its way into his voice as he proceeded with his narrative, compelled the young man to believe he was listening to a true tale. It was all very strange. What connection could Butler have with the story? The hero of it must be a very dear friend, or the shipbroker would not have been so deeply affected by the recital. Could it be that Butler was the hero of his own story ?

They were now near the garden gate of Woodbine Cottage. The elder man suddenly halted, and, turning towards the younger man, said,—

"I don't want you to brood too much over what I have told you. Forget the story itself, if you can ; but bear the moral attached to it in your memory."

Before Dalton could make any reply, both men heard behind them the sound of rapidly approaching footsteps and the rustle of a dress. In a moment Helen was at her uncle's side.

"You both deserve a scolding," she said. "Both Susan and I have been waiting for you at the gate for fully five minutes. She has sent me to fetch you in at once. And could you guess who is in the house, uncle ?"

"I am not very good at guessing," smiled Butler Then, with a frown, "I hope it is not Miss Walsh."

"No, thank goodness ! It is Mr Madden."

"Arthur !" cried Butler, with an uneasy start.

" What brings him here at such an hour, I wonder ? "

" I don't know, uncle. I suppose he wished to say good-bye to Susan. But I hope you are not going to stand here any longer. The air is growing chilly."

" Just a moment, dear. Tell Mrs M'Cormick we shall come directly."

" Very well, uncle. I shall depend on Captain Dalton to make you keep your word. Uncle sometimes grows so fond of studying the stars that it is impossible to move him."

" Unfortunately, Miss Cadogan," smiled Dalton, " there are no stars to study to night. Perhaps we shall have a peep at them by-and-by. I think it will rain very shortly."

" Yes," said Butler, gazing skywards, " we shall have rain—heavy rain, too, I fear. You had better get back to the house at once, Helen."

When Helen left them, Butler said,—

" I wonder what could bring Arthur here."

" Madden ! How can I tell ? "

Unintentionally, he spoke a little sharply. He had felt a pang of jealousy, which he was trying in vain to convince himself was wholly unjustifiable and silly. Could it be possible that Butler's good-looking clerk was in love with Susan? and might it not be that Susan was in love with him? Absurd! Still, try as he might to banish it, a jealous doubt clung to him. Madden was a devil-may-care fellow, who would push his suit with headlong recklessness: and was it not strange that for the second time he found Butler's clerk at Woodbine Cottage? Could it be possible that Susan was encouraging his visits? He must not harbour such•a thought.

Disgusted with himself, and kicking the ground impatiently, he turned towards Butler, with the intention of offering an apology for the ill-tempered manner in which he had spoken. The shipbroker had evidently forgotten he was not alone.

With his head thrown slightly back, he stood gazing at the sky, and Dalton observed that his lips were trembling, as if he were trying to repress some violent emotion.

The younger man somehow dreaded to disturb the reveries of the elder man. Melancholy is as often as contagious as laughter, and Dalton felt terribly depressed as he glanced in silence at his friend. Then he bent his head slightly and stared straight in front of him.

Over the roofs of the Bankside stores could be seen a narrow, lurid belt of river at the Sloughford side. The black hulls of the ships which lined the quays stood out like silhouettes against the lower part of the town, and through the spars and rigging the lights on the quay struggled feebly. Over the spars the lights on the hillside twinkled ; and over the town hung a luminous haze.

Slowly Dalton turned round until he faced the north. Then the dim outline of the bridge arrested his wandering gaze, and, full of bitter thoughts, he lifted his eyes from the bridge. The clouds were sluggish and low-lying ; but in the north-west, behind Yellow Hill, a faint, pale light lit up the sky. Again his eyes sought the bridge, and in a moment he addressed Butler abruptly,—

"I think we had better get indoors, Mr Butler. There is a break in the sky on the north-west. The wind is going to shift into that quarter directly, and we shall have heavy rain."

He had scarcely spoken when the raindrops came pattering to the ground. Both men hurried towards the house.

When they entered they found Madden had been doing his best to amuse the ladies. Consciously or unconsciously, Madden never entered into five minutes' conversation without relating some anecdote, more or less funny, concerning his own savings or doings. He had just been telling some stories — invented for the occasion — about Nixon.

Susan had at first tacitly declined to enjoy Madden's anecdotes. The mention of the *Greenback* distressed her, and she could not understand the want of taste which Butler's clerk exhibited in introducing any reference to the New Brunswicker. Then she saw that he had actually forgotten the connection between the *Greenback* and her affairs, and how could she blame him for his forgetfulness? Moreover, it was impossible to resist Madden when he had once made up his mind to be amusing, and Mrs M'Cormick soon —though she hated herself for doing so—joined in

Helen's and Madden's laughter, for Madden always laughed loudest at his own jokes.

Dalton was surprised to see that a great change had taken place in Susan's manner and appearance; and though her laughter was faint, and had a hollow ring, it jarred upon his ears. She looked utterly unlike the pale-faced woman who had startled him by her entrance into Butler's drawing-room a short time previously. Could the change be owing to Madden's presence?

Butler shook Madden's hand, and said,—

"Well, Arthur, what brings you this way to-night?"

"I was over at Bankside, sir, about that Sunderland brig, and I thought as I was so near Woodbine Cottage I ought to run up and say 'Good-bye' to Mrs M'Cormick."

It struck Dalton that it was not a little strange the shipbroker should have greeted his clerk, whom he met almost every day in the year, with a handshake; but he put the action down to Butler's good-nature—a desire on his part to put Madden quite at his ease.

Susan and Helen had moved to the window, and

now sat listening to the heavy patter of the rain against the glass. The men stood together near the fireplace, and after some desultory conversation, Dalton rose and went towards the window. The blinds were up, and Mrs M'Cormick had drawn back the curtains. Looking at the sky, Dalton, addressing himself to Susan, said,—"I think the rain has almost ceased. The nor'-wester is chasing the clouds helter-skelter before it. What do you say if we go outside and enjoy the air and the view?" And lowering his voice, "I fancy, Miss Cadogan, your uncle and Mr Madden have something to say to each other about business."

The ladies rose, and Dalton, raising his voice slightly, said,—"Mr Butler, we three are going into the garden to have a peep at the night. You will excuse us, won't you? The proposal is mine, so I have taken it upon myself to make the apology."

When Dalton opened the hall door, he found the rain had not quite ceased.

"I am afraid I have been too rash," he smiled "but the shower will soon be over. How refreshing the air here is!"

Helen proposed that they should stand in the porch until the rain had cleared off, and Susan made no objection; so they stood looking at the opposite side of the river almost in silence.

When Butler found himself alone with Madden, he began,—

"I am so sorry we missed the bank this afternoon. I have always a morbid fear of leaving money in the office at night."

"Don't trouble your head about it, sir. What could happen to it?"

"Who was the last in the office this evening?"

Madden started, and answered in a hesitating manner,—

"I was—at least," with a short, uneasy laugh, "I locked the place up under the impression I was."

"Sure you locked the safe?"

"Quite sure, sir."

"I know it is a trifle absurd on my part to feel uneasy about that money, but it is the first time I have ever left a large sum in the office at night."

"I wish you wouldn't trouble about it. Oh, I

had almost forgotten to tell you, sir. It is easy to account now for the delay about discharging the *Atalanta's* cargo. There is a strange rumour afloat this evening about Sutcliffe."

"What is it?"

"They say he has disappeared."

"Disappeared?"

"Well, absconded is the better word, perhaps."

"You astonish me. Is there any reason alleged?"

"It is supposed he found himself in difficulties, and didn't care to face his creditors. But I fancy that there is something more than mere bankruptcy at the bottom of it."

"This won't be very good news for the captain of the *Atalanta*. How does he stand with Sutcliffe?"

"I think he has drawn the greater part of his freight already, and he ought to have sufficient cargo still on board to cover the remainder. Perhaps we had better ask him about it."

"Don't upset him to-night, Arthur. He is not in very good spirits, I fancy. We can tell him in the morning. Nothing will be gained by disturbing his mind now. You're quite sure the money was all right in the safe when you locked up ?"

" Quite sure, sir."

" By Jove! it is much later than I thought. Has the rain cleared off, Arthur ?"

Madden rose and went to the window.

" Yes, I think the rain has ceased. The wind is very high—quite a little gale ! "

" I had better call Helen, and tell her we must be starting for home immediately."

He rose from his chair, and, advancing towards the open door of the room, he called his niece's name.

" I suppose you are coming with us, Arthur ?"

" Yes, sir."

Helen now entered the room. She was mischievously anxious to leave Mrs M'Cormick and Dalton alone for a few minutes, and her uncle's summons afforded her the opportunity she had been seeking. She saw that Susan's high spirits had again deserted her, and she was convinced her friend's melancholy had something to do with Dalton's departure—the *Atalanta* would be sailing from Sloughford in about a week, and it was not likely that Susan and her old lover would meet again. Therefore, when she entered the room she determined to find some pretext for making a short delay there in company with her uncle and Madden.

For some moments after Helen left them, neither Dalton nor Mrs M'Cormick seemed inclined to talk. Then, feeling that the silence was awkward, Dalton spoke. His voice was low and full of sadness.

"I suppose I shall not see you again for a long time. I wonder shall I ever see you again?"

"How can I tell? Life is full of changes."

So wrapt was he in his own melancholy, that he had not observed the alteration in Susan's voice and manner since she had come out into the porch; nor could he see, in the dim light, that her cheeks were no longer bright, her dark eyes dull and lustreless.

"I am glad to find you in good spirits on this the last night I may see you for years and years; and yet I am not altogether glad. There is a good deal of selfishness in my nature, I fear. Mr Madden seems to amuse you."

"Sometimes," she sighed. "I have been in a

strangely fickle mood to-day, and why I cannot
tell, except it is that the prospect of a change
from these dull walls behind us has lifted a weight
from my heart. This morning I felt that nothing
on earth could drive away my gloomy thoughts;
but I am always either unreasonably happy or
unreasonably miserable."

"And in which mood are you at this moment,
may I ask?"

"The melancholy mood. Oh! I am growing
old and irritable, I suppose. But why should I
trouble you about my tantrums? Let us find
some more interesting subjects for conversation
— the weather, for instance," she added, with a
faint laugh.

He looked at her in a startled way. Yes, she
was changed. What could have caused the
change?

"It is quite fine now," he said gently, holding
out his hand and gazing at the sky. "Let us
walk as far as the gate. The freshness of the air
will revive you."

They stepped out of the porch and walked down
the garden path.

"I am a regular weather-glass myself," said Dalton, endeavouring to divert Susan from introspection. "Until the clouds were chased from the sky by this glorious breeze, I was as depressed as a man could wish to be; now I feel quite boyish. How I love a good nor'-wester! It has blown years out of my life to-night."

Mrs M'Cormick was silent. Her thoughts were gradually wandering back to the olden time.

"I can scarcely realise," continued Dalton, in a tender tone, "that I am about to say good-bye to you. Why must it be always good-bye?"

He had forgotten the present; once more he was with the past; and he was addressing the woman at his side as if nothing had occurred to disturb the course of the old love, as if the impassable barrier of her marriage had never been raised. She felt there was some strange change in his voice and manner, and she trembled violently.

"How chilly it has grown!" she said, shrugging her shoulders. "We must return to the house at once." She spoke in as cold and as quiet a tone of voice as she could command. "What will my guests think of me for having neglected them? It is very stupid of me."

She turned to walk back to the house.

Dalton swiftly caught her hands.

"Susie! Susie!" he cried. "Is this to be our good-bye? Our parting years ago would have been a cold one but for you, my love, my love. We are going to part again, perhaps for ever. Have you nothing to say to me—no word I can carry with me?"

"I do not understand you. Let us go back. You forget."

She did not withdraw her hands; nor could she tell why she allowed them to remain clasped in his. She felt completely dazed. All she knew was that his eyes were looking into hers with a wild, tender, wistful gaze, and that the old love, for years a slumbering fire, had burst into flame within her. She tried to collect her thoughts, to rush madly away from the danger; but she could not utter a word, and her limbs were powerless. He felt her hands trembling violently within his own, and he saw that her cheeks were deadly white, that her bosom heaved convulsively. Scarcely knowing what he did, he seized her in his arms and kissed her lips passionately.

His kisses sent the blood into her cheeks and recalled her wandering senses. With a quick, angry movement she freed herself from his embrace.

At that moment Butler's figure stood out in the porch.

CHAPTER X.

A BURGLARY.

BUTLER'S office was opened every morning at eight o'clock by Foxy Ned. At nine Madden and Ryan were expected to be at their respective desks. Butler usually arrived a little before ten o'clock.

On the night of his visit to Woodbine Cottage the shipowner had been quite restless. A sum of money, about a hundred and forty pounds in gold, had been placed in his hands by the master of a ship after bank hours, and was lying in the office safe. As he had declared to Madden, he entertained a morbid fear of leaving money in the office at night. It sometimes had happened that he had received large sums in the evening, and it had always been his habit to take the money to his dwelling-house;

but on this occasion Madden had pooh-poohed the notion of there being any danger in leaving money in the office, and Butler had decided to leave the gold in the safe.

The next morning he rose early, and without disturbing his household he left Prince's Street about half-past seven, and soon found himself standing outside his office door. With a sigh of relief he took a door-key from his pocket and put it into the keyhole. As he did so the door opened slightly. Astonished and alarmed — he knew he had not turned the key in the lock—he pushed the door open and entered the passage. He stooped and examined the lock. There appeared to be nothing the matter with it. "How very stupid of Arthur," he thought, "to leave the door unlocked! It gave me quite a fright. He shall have a sound railing for his negligence."

He walked up the passage, and as his eyes grew more accustomed to the dim light in the passage, he saw that the back door was slightly open. He also noticed that the doors of the two offices, usually closed at night, were wide open. He advanced hastily towards the end of the passage, and almost with the same glance saw the position of affairs in Madden's office and in Ryan's.

The floors were littered with papers and books. Desks were thrown open and drawers were scattered about in every direction.

He entered Madden's office. There were no shutters to the windows in either office. A yellow linen blind which admitted the daylight was drawn down every evening, and the windows were protected on the outside by horizontal iron bars. There was sufficient light to see plainly what had happened during the night. The door of the safe had been forced open, and its contents were scattered on the floor. The two interior drawers of the safe were lying on the floor, bottom upwards; one drawer had held the gold; in the other M'Cormick's tin box had been placed.

Fearful lest some one might still be lurking on the premises he quickly drew up the window-blind; the dim yellow light was changed to a bright white light, which found its way into every nook and cranny in the office. He then crossed the passage and drew up the blind in Ryan's office. Here the litter and confusion were greater than in Madden's office. Butler had to walk almost ankle deep in papers and books in order to reach the window. After drawing up the blind he saw that some of the upturned drawers on the ground had been completely smashed. "The thieves lost their temper here, I suppose," he muttered, "and finding nothing worth stealing, vented their displeasure on my unoffending property." He had no doubt about the gold; he was quite convinced it had been the object of the burglary. Nevertheless he returned to Madden's office and turned up the iron drawer in which the money had been deposited. As he expected, the gold was gone. His eye now caught, in a distant corner of the office, the glitter of the tin box which held M'Cormick's will. He picked his way leisurely through the litter on the floor and picked up the case.

An expression of alarm came into his face. The padlock had been opened, and the case was empty.

For almost a minute he stood motionless. Then with a smile he walked to the safe, and placing M'Cormick's case on the top of the safe, he reflected :—

"How stupid of me to be so much alarmed! No doubt the will is somewhere on the ground. Why should a burglar trouble his head about a piece of parchment ? I must have a search for it immediately."

He walked out of the office, locking the door after him, and advanced down the passage. As he came to the front door a man, entering the office hurriedly, stumbled against him.

"Beg pardon, sir," said Foxy Ned, astonished to find his master in the office at such an hour. "I'm a thrifle behind time, I know; but it won't occur again, sir; it won't occur again. The fact is—"

"Go round at once to the Prince's Street Police Barracks, and fetch a constable here."

"A constable, sir!" cried Ned, in alarm. "You wrong me, sir. There was never a man served you more faithful and honest all these years than my own self, Mr Butler. I hope you don't believe I'd do a dirty turn against you, sir."

Ned's mind was, and had been for some days, wholly occupied in the concoction of a small swindle, and he was unable to divest himself of the notion that the shipbroker could see into the innermost workings of his brain.

"I don't quite understand you, Ned," said Butler, with a quiet smile; "unless it is that you are suffering from a guilty conscience. The office has been broken into during the night."

"Broken into, sir! Glory be to heaven! you don't say so! Broken into!"

In his astonishment he forgot the respect he owed to his employer, and he rushed past him into the office. Butler saw him dart into Ryan's office, and in a few moments Ned was again at the front door, his face the picture of surprise and vexation.

"Shocking, sir! Shocking!" he cried. "I'll run round to the barracks this minute. Broken into! There's no mistake about it, sir; it must have been a desperate gang that did it—a desperate, bloodthirsty gang."

"Don't stand chattering there. Be off at once, like a good man."

Ned hobbled away, breaking into a gentle trot as he advanced. The disastrous nature of the burglary had come home to him with peculiar force. In a disused cupboard in Ryan's office Ned usually kept a certain black bottle, and when he went into the office he found the bottle on the floor—empty.

Butler went back to Madden's office and commenced the search for the will. He had not been many minutes so engaged when Foxy Ned returned, in company with a stout, red-faced sergeant of police.

" I brought the sergeant himself, sir," said Ned breathlessly. " If there's a man in the country that can ferret out a thief or a blackguard, the sergeant is that man. He's the grandest—"

" That will do, Ned. Go out and stand at the door until I have a few words privately with your friend."

Butler then informed the policeman, who made entries in his note-book of all the salient facts, what he knew concerning the condition of affairs in the office the previous evening, and the condition of them when he had entered the premises at half-past seven o'clock. So full were his thoughts of the will that he forgot to make any mention of the gold which had been in the safe.

" But what could be the object of breaking into a place like this?" asked the policeman. " It is well known you don't keep money here."

" But there was money here last night."

" Much ? "

" A hundred and forty pounds in gold, and some loose silver in the cash-box—two or three pounds, I think."

" Phew ! " whistled the sergeant. " That alters
the view of the case. Let us first discover how
the entry was effected. The motive is plain enough
now."

The two men went into the pasasge.

" Back door forced in," said the sergeant, examining the door. " Lock smashed, and bolt filed through.
It was the bolt that the difficulty was with," looking
at Butler ; " the lock wasn't worth three-halfpence.
'Entry effected through the backyard from the
outside,' making an entry in his notebook. No
doubt about that, I think."

" How on earth could the entry be effected from
the inside ? " asked Butler.

" I don't know, I'm sure," replied the sergeant,
with a cunning twinkle in his eyes.

Butler was puzzled. " Stupid fellow ! " he thought.

" Now, sir," said the sergeant, " let us have a
look at the front door. No force used here evidently," he observed, stooping down and examining
the lock and the iron staple in the jamb of the
door, into which the lock-bolt fitted. " Lend me
your key, Mr Butler."

The shipbroker took the key from his pocket,

and the sergeant put it into the keyhole, and, turning the key, shot out the bolt.   Giving the bolt
a push with the palm of his hand, he forced the bolt
easily back. " No difficulty about this lock either.
You see a child could have forced it. Might I ask,
sir, who was the last to leave the office last night
—who locked it up ? "

" My confidential clerk."

" Mr Madden ? "

" Yes."

" Ah ! "

" What's the matter, sergeant ? "

" Nothing, sir.   Now let us see if we can find
any clue to the thieves. Was it commonly known
about this money in the safe ? "

" No.   At least I am not aware that anyone
knew I had kept it in the office except my two
clerks."

" Mr Madden and Mr Ryan ? "

" Yes."

" Well, if you don't object, I'll make an exami-
nation of Mr Madden's office with you."

" I wish you would, sergeant ; and if you could
help me to discover a document which was taken

out of my safe, I promise you will not regret having found it."

"All right, sir. Was the document a valuable one—I mean could it by any plan be converted into hard cash?"

"No. It was of no value in the sense you mean, sergeant. What a dreadful litter the place is in!"

"Was the gold loose?"

"No; it was tied up in a small canvas bag. I am not in so much trouble about the gold. That can be replaced; but the parchment cannot."

For upwards of half-an-hour the police-sergeant and Butler searched the floor for the missing document. Butler could not tell what shape or size the will was; but he was confident the material on which it was drafted was parchment. He knew that nautical folk as a rule believed a document was worthless from a legal point of view unless it were drawn upon parchment. Therefore he desired the policeman to confine his efforts to sorting out from the medley of documents on the floor any parchments he might meet. This simplified matters considerably, and before nine o'clock Butler had made up his mind the will had been stolen. There were ten parchments on the desk—six certificates of registry, three certificates of classification, and the Bishop's certificate of competency.

"Let us go into the other office now," said Butler. "Perhaps you had better have a look round there, and then I suppose you will examine the yard at the back before you make a report."

"Yes; I am very sorry our search has been unsuccessful, sir. Might I ask you another question? How many people knew where this document you have been looking for was locked up?"

"I am not aware that anyone alive, except myself, knew that case," pointing to M'Cormick's tin box, "was locked up in the safe. This," pointing with his foot to an upturned iron drawer on the floor, "was a private drawer of mine."

"The very place, of course, anyone would naturally conclude you would keep an important document."

"Granted; but I don't see what light that throws upon your part of the business, which is, I presume, to catch the thieves."

"I am not so sure of that."

"How? What do you mean?"

" Oh, nothing, sir. Had we not better examine the other office ? "

When the two men entered Ryan's office, the quick eye of the policeman caught sight of a small bundle lying under the desk. Going down on his knees, he drew the bundle out, and, slowly rising, he placed it on the desk.

" A burglar's kit ! " he cried, opening out what seemed to the shipbroker a small piece of carpet. " Look here, Mr Butler, isn't that beautiful ? I haven't seen anything half so neat since I joined the force."

The shipbroker could not see any beauty in the tools now laid out for his inspection. Indeed, one of them, a long, heavy chisel, with a large gap in the end of it, sent a thrill of horror through him.

" Roll that thing up, sergeant."

The policeman tenderly wrapped up the collection of bright skeleton keys and dull jemmies, and then his spell of ecstasy was over. With a frown he said,—

" This puts a new aspect on the case. Those tools were never made in Sloughford. My suspicions are all knocked on the head—unless," he 'added, as if to himself, " the kit was left here as a blind."

" I don't understand you. What were those wonderful suspicions of yours, sergeant ? "

" Suspicions ! " exclaimed the policeman, with well-feigned astonishment. " I have no suspicions—not yet, at any rate."

" But a moment ago you said you had."

" A mistake, sir. Quite a mistake of mine if I did say so."

" Stupid man ! " reflected Butler again. " I wish a less conceited member of the force had been sent here."

It was now about a quarter after nine, and Foxy Ned, who was standing outside the office door, saw Madden and Ryan approaching leisurely arm-in-arm. He ran to meet them.

" Shocking work, Mr Arthur ! Shocking work, Mr Michael ! " he exclaimed.

" What is it ? " asked both men, standing still.

" The office has been broken into. The peelers are in the place. Such a mess you never saw."

" Broken into ! How do you mean ? What do you mean ? " cried Madden, his cheeks turning suddenly white.

" You'll see soon enough, sir. The back door

smashed open; the front door broke open; the safe and everything in it thrown about the floor. The master is inside himself, ready to tear his hair off; and no wonder."

"Let us hurry in, Madden. Don't stand there listening to Ned's gabble. You see the governor was right about not leaving money in the place."

"Hold on a minute. Ned gave me such a devil of a shock. I thought at first something might have happened to the governor. Now," heaving a deep sigh, "I am ready."

"I expect you will find Ned has been drawing the long bow a little," said Ryan, as the two men hurried towards the office.

"I hope—I mean, I think not. He hasn't the imagination to invent a back and front door smashed open, not to mention a safe thrown all over the floor."

END OF VOL. I.